FINDING WHAT WE LOST

Sanna Hines

This is a work of fiction. The events and characters described herein are imaginary and are not intended to refer to specific places or living persons.

Finding What We Lost

ISBN: 978-0-9994339-6-6

For Alisa, Victor, and Phyllis

1.

My mother packed hastily for the flight from Florida to Maine. "Megan, you'll follow tomorrow," she said, "after you pick up your father's medication." She blew air through exasperated lips. "You'd think they could speed up these prescriptions in an emergency, but no. No, *they* have to have time. Time is just what we don't have! The first forty-eight hours after an abduction is critical. Why can't they understand that?"

I couldn't answer her. I was still reeling from the idea I'd be inhabiting Great-Aunt Dotty's house in Maine. I hated that house. "We don't know if she was abducted."

"No," Mom admitted. "She might have wandered off. Poor thing is in her seventies now and—"

"She doesn't have both feet on the ground at the best of times," I finished. By choice, Aunt Dotty dwelt in the year 1910. She wore the clothes; lived the life. After her husband died, she retreated to the last century, what she called the Age of Innocence.

Instead of getting annoyed with my criticism of her beloved aunt, Mom sat, head in hands, on the bed beside her suitcase. "I'm just so…so worried," she muttered. Looking up, she asked, "Where could she have gone? There's nothing but a couple houses on the island. The town on the mainland is tiny. You don't think she forgot the time and the tide…."

"Not a problem," I said. "The tide didn't get her. Police found her bicycle in the town's cemetery. She wouldn't just leave it there and walk home. Besides, the causeway connecting the island to the mainland is submerged at high tide. Even Dotty wouldn't walk into waves."

"True. Someone must have taken her, but who'd want my aunt?"

"Treasure hunters thinking she had the inside track on pirate loot buried on the island? Spies? Remember her husband's Secret Room with the false passports, foreign currencies and weapons?"

Mom waved that off. "He was a diplomat. That's all."

"Who got car bombed in, uh, one of those -stan countries."

"Kazakhstan. Just bad luck. Anyway, Thomas died some thirty years ago. Why would spies wait so long?" Mom left the bed to get underwear from her dresser. "I'm thinking Dotty may be lost. You know old people can forget where they are when…when they get dementia. Maybe she doesn't know who she is or how to get home. The police force is small. They can't devote full time to searching for her."

Mom pitched the clothes she held into the suitcase and shut it, yanking the zipper with too much zeal. It caught on the fabric. Staring at the jam, she cried, "Damn. Dammit all!"

I moved her aside to fix the problem, then took her shoulders in hand. "We'll find her. You and Dad are going to canvass the neighborhood—"

"The town, and then the next," my mother vowed, eyes glistening with unshed tears. "We'll search the whole coast of Maine if we have to."

I smiled and released her. Mom might be more amenable to my idea when she was in fighting fettle. "I'll hold down the fort, though, um, maybe I could stay on the mainland? There must be a B&B somewhere nearby."

"Whatever for?"

"You know I get claustrophobic in that house, where every square inch is covered with *stuff.* I mean, she has stuff on top of stuff. It's creepy."

"Oh." Mom sighed. "I thought you'd outgrown that phase. Come on, Megan, you're a woman, not a child. Furniture and what-nots aren't going to attack you."

"What about the secret room, the weird cistern, footsteps on the stairs—the *ghost*?"

"They haven't bothered Dotty, so I'm sure you'll be fine. Besides, I need you to do an inventory of her collections."

"Me?" I squeaked. "I don't know what she has." I tilted my head as a mean thought took over my tongue. "Why are you worried about her possessions? Are you planning to sell them?"

"Yes," my mother said, shocking me to the core. "If needs be. If Dotty has, well, lost her mind, she'll require round-the-clock care. Good care costs money. We can't sell the house because she'd be heartbroken. She owns some stock, I believe, but it's not the time to sell shares. Her collections…. Dotty doesn't even use them. Most are packed in crates. What better purpose can they have than paying for her caregivers? Oh, I wish we could bring her here, but it just wouldn't work." Mom held up helpless hands.

I agreed with her. "Dotty would hate Florida, hate the heat, the parched vegetation, the flat sameness of buildings designed for everywhere and nowhere. It's not Maine."

Truth be told, I had no great love for the state my parents migrated to after Dad retired. He was delighted with his golf and his swimming pool, his certainty of never seeing another snowflake. My mother, seven years younger, kept busy selling real estate. I hid beneath hats, sunblock and SPF clothing. Florida sun fricassees redheads.

A moment's reflection made me realize paying out of pocket for Dotty's caregivers could strain my parents' resources. Their finances seemed solid enough for their needs, but now they had me on their hands. After a failed marriage, I'd come creeping back to Mom and Dad, mostly broke and completely unemployed.

"I need to keep job hunting," I argued.

"And how will you do that?"

"Uh, the Internet, I guess."

"You can search in Maine as well as Florida.

"Aunt Dotty won't have wi-fi."

"Her tenant has it. I called him to let him know you were coming."

"Then why can't he keep an eye out for Dotty?"

"He's in and out—telecommutes some days, works in Portland on others. I need you on the island full time. And," she added, eyeing me severely, "there's the inventory."

As I nodded my reluctant head, Dad came into the bedroom. "We about ready?"

"I think so. Anything I've forgotten we'll buy," Mom said. "Megan's set to take the flight tomorrow."

"You have enough cash?" Dad asked me. I told him I had a credit card, but he pressed a wad of bills in my hand. "Just in case."

After hugs all around, I watched my parents depart. In the condo's living room, I sank down on the couch and wondered how long I'd be marooned on an island in Maine. I wanted Dotty found: for all her eccentricities, she was a kind, sweet person. In large part, she'd raised my mother.

I hoped she was safe, wherever she was. And I hoped she'd come home soon—really soon.

2.

Eyelids squeezed shut, teeth clenched, fingers strangling the plane's armrests, I took shallow, rapid breaths as we climbed to cruising altitude. I released my white-knuckled hold only when the pilot predicted we'd have clear air up the coast. He turned off the seatbelt sign. I kept my belt on.

I've always been a gutless flyer. There's something horrible about being trapped in a metal tube. I feel like an animal captive in a livestock trailer. Captive…was Aunt Dotty captive? A prisoner somewhere?

Shuddering at the thought, I focused on facts. What did I know about my great-aunt? I'd visited her on the island often when I was a child, less often as an adolescent and not at all as an adult. Last time I'd seen Dotty was eight years ago at my wedding. She appeared in an emerald suit with short, scalloped jacket and long skirt, both trimmed with interlaced turquoise braid. High-necked, lacy white blouse, as always. Wide, green hat with gauzy silk ribbon and a peacock eye feather. Parasol, pearls, cameo and gloves. I watched the wedding guests struggle to take their eyes off Dotty when I made my entrance on my father's arm.

This was no surprise. Apart from her costume, Dotty was a stunning woman even in her sixties, as she was then. Tall and slender, she exuded a kind of grace that bordered on regal. Her upswept hair had lost the carrot tone of youth, fading to a reddish-blonde. My mother said Dotty used henna to revive her color and banish gray. If so, it didn't quite work along her temples, where loose blonde curls softened the edges of her face.

Dotty probably still had that suit. She came from a family of savers.

Dorothy Ann Whitcomb (always called Dot or Dotty) grew up in Brunswick, Maine with parents and an older sister named Julie. Her father was a doctor, so the family lived in a sizable, turn-of-the-century house. A good student, Dotty earned a college degree and education credentials, returning to Brunswick to teach high school history.

"Oh, how my grandmother wanted her to marry!" Mom told me one day. "Dotty had boyfriends, lots of them, but they always parted, sometimes by her choice, sometimes by theirs. When Dotty hit thirty-four, Grandmother gave up match-making, declaring, 'My daughter doesn't need a man to complete her.' I don't know if she believed that, but it was a way to save face. If only she'd lived past 1984, she'd have seen Dotty married."

The year after her mother died, Dotty took an adventure tour to hike the hills of Turkey and visit ancient ruins. A fellow traveler arrived with two bodyguards: one Turk, one American. Dotty suspected Thomas Hartley was a criminal until one night around the campfire she learned he was a diplomat, a widower with a grown son, and he hailed from Hopewell—"just spittin' distance from Brunswick," he teased when she told him where she taught school. This connection turned to friendship and then to love. They were married in Brunswick three days after the tour ended.

My plane bounced. I shrieked. People turned to stare at me. *Don't think about flying. Don't think about nothing but air between you and the ground.* With a deep breath, I took my own advice.

Dotty. Where was I? Ah, yes. She'd married Thomas. They moved to Spear Point and were happy, even when saddled with other people's children.

The first of these was my mother, Dotty's niece, after my grandmother died of cancer. Mom was six when her father panicked about having no one to look after his child during the summer. He could cope with the school year, but what to do with those long, unsupervised days? Send her to Dotty. And so, Mom went to Maine each summer for the next twelve years.

Dotty and Thomas enjoyed her presence, Mom said, "I suppose because they had no children together." They didn't complain to her father, and they didn't stop the visits, so Mom was probably right. Surely, after Thomas died in '91, my mom must have been welcome company.

After Mom grew up, Thomas' grandson, Tyler, was sent to Dotty each summer, starting in 2001. "He was a handful," my mother confided. "Chatting with Dotty, I learned his parents thought he'd stay out of trouble if restricted to Spear Point." Tyler viewed his teenaged stays as prison. He regained his freedom in 2007, when he turned eighteen.

Though I'd visited for weeks at a time accompanying my mother on her annual pilgrimage to Dotty's, I didn't pay much attention to Tyler until I was thirteen, a summer-long guest in 2007. That was the year my parents took an all-expenses-paid trip to London for a conference where my dad got an award. Those expenses didn't cover my little brother, Eliot, or me. Eliot went to camp, but I flatly refused—all right, I screamed and raised hell—at the idea of living in dank woods surrounded by mosquitos, ticks, spiders and snakes. Nuh uh. Not me.

Since then, what happened in Dotty's life? I realized I didn't know anything about her recent years. Had she made enemies evil enough to kidnap her? Had she, as Mom feared, truly gone 'round the bend? I didn't want to believe either of these scenarios, but what other options were there? I wouldn't know until I got to Maine. Then, I'd do some serious digging.

The three-hour flight dragged on. I flipped through the onboard magazine, fiddled with my phone and tried to nap. At long last, we neared the airport. I went through my usual landing terror until the wheels touched down.

Portland International Jetport is a pleasant place—not too big, not too crowded. I found the baggage area, and wonder of wonders! My bag was the first one on the carousel. Heading for the outside doors, I expected to find my parents in their rental car waiting in the cell-phone lot. I texted Mom, who didn't answer. Huh.

Someone called my name, and I spotted a sign: Megan Fields. I was using my maiden name again, but it still felt awkward, took a moment to process.

Looking at the man behind the sign, my eyes narrowed. "Tyler Hartley?" *Tyler the vain.* He didn't rank highest on my least-favorite-person-in-the-world list—that was my ex-husband—but Tyler made the top five. "What are you doing here?"

"I'm your ride. Your mother strong-armed me into it."

"Since when do you take orders from my mother?"

"Since I was working in Portland and ready to leave for Spear Point anyway."

I nodded. He sounded sufficiently self-absorbed. One awful thought popped up. "Why are you going to the island?"

"I live there."

"*You're* Aunt Dotty's tenant?"

"Sort of. She owns the land; I own the cottage. My grandmother gave it to Dad, who gave it to me."

Grandmother. I'd nearly forgotten Tyler was Dotty's step-grandson. He'd always called her The Warden when we were kids.

We eyed each other. He still had the roguish smile, and there it was—the twinkle in his eyes that showed up when he was amused. He must be amused to see me ogling him. Same light eyes and thick, dark hair. If anything, Tyler looked better than when he was a teen—filled out, less gangly, more solid. It wasn't fair.

"Wow," he said. "How long's it been—fifteen years? You're all grown up."

"Seventeen. And, yeah, life happens."

Tyler shoved the sign into the pocket of his sports jacket and gestured toward my suitcase. "Want me to take that?"

"It's on wheels. I can manage."

"Fine, but let's get a move on if you don't want to spend six hours on shore waiting for the tide to recede."

I did some rapid calculations. If we made good time, it'd take around an hour to reach Hopewell, the town nearest the island. Wait there for another six hours in some café with insufferable Tyler? No, just no. I scuttled toward the airport doors.

At the curb, I stopped, turning to Tyler. "Wait a minute. You said we could drive to Spear Point. How? Aunt Dotty doesn't allow modern cars."

"I found a way." Tyler added his infuriating grin. "Follow me."

His car was parked a couple football fields away, but when we found it, I understood. "Electric car!"

"Yeah. Dotty didn't object to it, though she makes me park it in the shed so as not to ruin the view."

Next thing he did surprised me: he opened my door. It'd been so long since a man opened a door for me, I was stunned into silence.

Before climbing inside, he took off his jacket and laid it neatly on the back seat. I was surprised again when we started rolling but I heard no engine start-up noise. The car was amazingly quiet.

As was I. I didn't want to distract Tyler while he negotiated the maze of the parking lot and route to the Turnpike, but I shouldn't have worried: he knew the way. Once we were cruising 295, I could wait no longer. "What do you know about Dotty's disappearance?"

"Nothing, damn it!" He scowled and shook his head. "I left early on Tuesday. First I heard was when the police phoned. After they spotted her bike in the cemetery, they looked around, found nothing, canvassed nearby houses, then called me. I thought maybe her bike broke, so she went off to find someone to help. But they said the bike ran fine; they tested it. I told them to call your mother. Dotty goes to the general store to call your mother every Tuesday. She likes their old-fashioned phone there."

"Not this Tuesday," I said. "And how did they know the bike was hers?"

"Pedaling to Hopewell was getting hard on her. I found a reproduction friction-drive, electric bicycle kit. Perfectly 1910. No one else in town has anything like it."

"Do you think her mind could be wandering? Maybe she's forgotten who she is."

"Nah. She's still sharp as a tack. There's some other reason why she's gone. But we'll find her. I'm taking time off work to search."

Who was this thoughtful, generous man, and what had he done to Tyler Hartley?

"What's your schedule?" Tyler asked. "How long will you be here?"

I shrugged. "I'm unemployed. My time is my own. I can stay as long as I'm needed."

"Heard you got married. Won't hubby complain?"

"Ex-hubby," I told him. "So, no."

Tyler groaned. "You're not gonna spend the rest of the trip boring me with the hundred and one ways the guy's a dick, are you?"

Ah, *there* was the old Tyler. Never afraid to trample my feelings. "Wouldn't dream of it. It's none of your business."

"Right. Tunes?" Without waiting for my answer, he fiddled with the display screen, settling on country-rock. Not my favorite.

I busied myself with my phone, looking up info on Casco Bay and its fringe of rocky peninsulas reaching down from north to south like skeletal fingers. Someone estimated there were two hundred islands among the peninsulas.

North of Falmouth, our route took us near enough the Atlantic to see deep blue water and cloudless sapphire sky. Then on past Freeport and up to Brunswick, where I heard from my mother, who said they were in town to search around Dotty's childhood neighborhood in case she decided to visit old friends. So far, no luck. Mom said they'd stay in Brunswick overnight and advised me to continue to Spear Point.

Tyler turned onto a small road that tunneled through pines and oaks. When the road forked, he asked "What time is it?"

"2:40"

"Tide's out. We hit it right."

Trees gave way to shore and the stony area we called a causeway, though there was nothing manmade about it. Tyler's car had all-wheel drive. *Good thing*, I thought, as we jounced over the uneven rocky track that finally rose past the high-water mark of the peninsula. Though we called Spear Point an island, the description only fit when the tide was in.

I barely observed the other buildings because my eyes were

riveted on the house. It wasn't Gothic or spooky; to the contrary, the two- and a-half story frame structure looked fresh and bright. White with dark gray trim, Dotty's house wouldn't scare anyone but me, I suspected, as my claustrophobia blossomed while I recalled the parlor packed to the gunnels with furniture and bric-a-brac.

When I lived there the summer of '07, I always entered by the kitchen door to head up the back stairs. The second floor was less crammed, so I liked it better—during the daytime, at least. At night, not so much.

Tyler drove over the grass, parking beside the front steps. "I'll go in with you. Maybe Dotty's come home. Or maybe those treasure hunters came back. I'll know if anyone's been here."

"What treasure hunters?" I hoped the story was long so I could put off going inside.

"Guys from a ship landed their dinghy to ask Dotty if they could check out Spear Point. They're not the first. Last time, it was pirate gold the treasure hunters were after. This time, they wanted Viking artifacts."

"Viking? That's crazy."

"Yeah, I thought so, but they argued the current from Naskeag, where that Norwegian Maine Penny was found, to Spear Point could lead a ship here." Tyle shrugged. "Who knows? Anyway, Dotty sent them packing."

"Did you tell the cops this?"

"No point. A couple days later, the ship took off. Hasn't been seen since."

Tyler was at the door now. He pulled out a key and opened it. "After you." He stepped aside.

I took a steadying breath. The front door led to the staircase hall. Just left, was the dreaded parlor. When I looked in that direction, something was different. The room had more light. I moved through the doorway, and gasped. "Ohmygod! What's happened here?"

3.

My footsteps echoed in Dotty's empty parlor. Gone was the maroon carpet with its dizzying parade of golden medallions. Gone, too, were the puce funeral-parlor drapes, the tufted ottoman, the marble-topped chest and the gilded mirror hung at a looming angle so viewers looked short and squat. Nowhere in sight were the glowering portraits, the seascape of waves battering a doomed ship, the snarling pug dogs or any other dusty porcelains. Best of all, the shadowbox with the dead-ancestor hair wreath had been banished to someplace I hoped I'd never find.

In one corner, the fainting couch still loitered next to the whatnot shelf, which had shed its burden of ostrich egg, stuffed birds under glass, flaking photo albums and myriad picture frames. Only the steel-gray, horsehair sofa held onto its position by the fireplace. A slight end table hid beside it.

I whirled to face Tyler, who beamed like a beauty contest winner. Before I could stammer out my questions, he waved me toward the dining room door. "This way. The best is yet to come."

Passing the spot where once a monstrous, claw-foot table hunched over predatory chairs, I followed him toward Thomas' study. Dotty had preserved this shrine to her husband. As I remembered it, floor-to-ceiling bookshelves filled three walls. High, small windows let in light behind his desk.

Today all that remained in the room were the desk, desk chair, two standing lamps and a few books on one wall of shelves—the wall concealing Thomas' Secret Room. Everything else was gone.

"What," I enunciated slowly, "has happened to this house? Dotty never changed the décor after she inherited the place from Thomas. Why now?"

"Necessity," Tyler said. "Floors were sagging. Doors wouldn't close; windows wouldn't open. I did a stress analysis and told her either she should call in heavy equipment to replace floor joists and beams or off-load weight and see if the wood could recover enough to use jacks. Wood has remarkable elasticity. Dotty still balked until I reminded her, in this new century, people were turning to lighter, simpler furnishings. By new century, of course, I meant the Twentieth."

"You're a contractor?"

"Engineer."

"Nah. Can't be. That's precise work. You're too scatterbrained."

Tyler frowned. "What makes you an authority on me?"

"Just going on memory. Every time I took a walk outside, I'd spot abandoned sunglasses, ball caps, one flip-flop or a tee shirt."

"When I was a kid, yeah. Had things on my mind."

"All those girlfriends."

Tyler grinned. "Probably. The good old days."

"And now?"

He pulled out his phone. "Now I run into town to snag some groceries before the tide turns. Only edibles in my frig are mayonnaise and pickles. Wanna come?"

I shook my head. "I'm going to search the house for clues of where Dotty could have gone. Maybe she left herself a note or maybe there are signs of a struggle."

"Struggle—here? I don't get it. She went to visit Thomas in the cemetery before she vanished."

"Did she? We don't know for sure. Someone could have abducted her from this house, then left her bike in the cemetery to throw off police."

Tyler hmphed. "I never thought of that. I bet the cops didn't, either. We'll have to run the idea by them tomorrow when we do the full sweep of Hopewell." He consulted his phone again. "Low tide's at 4:01 a.m. General Store opens around 6:30 for fishermen and tourists making the drive south. We need to be back on Spear Point before 10:00, so be ready by 6:00."

I quaked inside. I'm a night owl, not an early bird. "Six it is," I confirmed with false heartiness.

After Tyler left, I retraced my steps through dining room, parlor and front hall, heading to Dotty's bedroom. Years ago, she renounced the second-floor master suite, refusing to hike up twelve stairs every time she wanted something from her room. Instead, she'd taken over the Morning Room, a space designed for lingering over coffee, reading the paper, writing letters and chatting with close friends. Of all the rooms in the house, I liked Dotty's bedroom best.

It was cheerful, papered with tiny, yellow rosebuds and warmed by sunlit windows. The wall facing the ocean held a nook with cushioned seat. I'd never holed up there with a book, but I'd often thought how cozy it would be.

Dotty's three-piece bedroom suit—She'd corrected me when I called it a set. "Not set, dear. It's properly called a suit."—consisted of bed with high headboard, a dresser with beveled mirror, and a wash stand. The stand was intended to hold basin, pitcher and towels. Dotty used the towel bar for her ribbons and belts, without which no lady of 1910 would leave her home.

She hadn't lightened the load in here very much. Still had two wardrobes for her clothing—Dotty loved clothes—and amber velvet drapes covering the tall, east-side windows. I guess she needed the drapes to block the rising sun and to preserve her privacy, as Tyler's cottage was just fifty feet or so away across the lawn, the only patch of tillable ground on Spear Point Dotty hadn't filled with flower and vegetable gardens.

I went to her desk, rolled up the top, and found recent bills plus a few letters—actual paper letters. I checked the postmarks. The dates were all from years ago, so I wouldn't find hints about recent plans to go anywhere. After a peek into the bath, I left Dotty's rooms, only to come to a dead stop in the hall.

Something was missing. The little tables and mirror had disappeared, but that wasn't what made me pause. It was the absence of the handmade oriental carpet padding the stairs. The steps still held brass carpet bars, though they no longer served a purpose. The staircase looked sad.

Dotty didn't spend much time upstairs, so I made quick work of checking that floor. To the left of the stair landing was the abandoned master suite, now a guest room. A glance inside showed me she'd left just enough furniture for visitors to use during their stay. "My" room—the former nursery across the hall—had lost one of its twin beds. Finally, the pocket-sized bathroom repurposed from a nanny's bedchamber held nothing of interest.

I parted the hall curtain and stepped down to the servants' floor level, purposely lower than the family quarters. There were two rooms and an attic—all empty. Where had Dotty's possessions gone? I pondered the question while descending the rear stairs to the laundry. On impulse I went out to the screen porch, then through the other door into the kitchen. Here, I would find something. I was sure of it. The kitchen was Dotty's domain.

The modern refrigerator was a shock. Dotty had used an icebox with block ice to keep food cold. Had the icebox given up the ghost or was it the old man who delivered the blocks?

No surprise Dotty still had the antique electric stove. This stood on curved legs, offered only two burners and a narrow box oven, yet she managed to bake an endless array of perfect bread, muffins, cakes, cookies and pies in that device.

I went to the pantry where, sometimes, Dotty left notes to herself on a cork board hung behind one door. Zero notes, and everything in order. Half of one pantry section was devoted to grains, more than a few of them exotic. I mean what do you do with spelts or amaranth? Above the crocks of grain were canned jars of fruits and veg from the garden. On the opposing shelves were cast iron cookware and vintage tools—things like a crank-handle apple peeler, a juice press, a scale plus weight-and-measure set, and a glass butter churn. I touched the churn. Dotty taught me the magic of turning cream and salt into luscious butter with that gadget.

Frustrated, not knowing what to do, I sat at the kitchen table, angrily shoving away the bread box in front of me. It was then I saw the vase of wilted flowers and a pie plate under a checkered cloth. I lifted the cloth. Around the prickings of the top crust, I spotted blueberry juice.

Dotty baked a pie and left it to cool. She expected to come home to taste it. She hadn't planned to go away. Someone had taken her from her pie, from her world. Had they taken her life, too? Would her body, thrown into the forest, be found by hikers in months or years to come?

I dropped my head onto my hands and wept.

When the front doorbell rang, I pulled myself together enough to greet Tyler, who stood holding a cloth sack of groceries. "Bread, eggs, milk, butter, o.j., hamburger, a cobb salad, lobster mac, mixed berries. Got a jar of peanut butter, too, in case you're gluten-free, vegan, or whatever. Man, it's hard to shop for people today, with all the weird diets. Keep the sack; you have to bring your own to the General Store. Oh, and I wrote down the WIFI password on a slip of paper." He stopped talking to scrutinize me. Surely, my puffy eyes gave me away. "You okay?"

"I'm fine. Thanks for the food. I'll repay you tomorrow." I took the sack and nodded. He took the hint and left.

My voice sounded normal, so I called my parents. When I heard Mom's upbeat tone, I didn't tell her about the pie, just let her ramble on. To get through this awful slack time without leads or news, Mom had to keep busy, feel she was doing something useful.

They were staying in Brunswick overnight, awaiting a visit in the morning to the school where Dotty taught. Mom wanted to check if teachers still working there might know her. Was any reunion of teachers or students scheduled? Slim chance of either, my mother admitted, but she wanted to leave no stone unturned.

After Brunswick, they were going to Wiscasset, where Dotty's best friend from high school lived. Dotty and Sally Wexford—now Sally Abbott—stayed in touch over the years. With some prompting, Sally might recall a smidge of helpful conversation with Dotty. Even an "I wish I could see…" would be a lead.

Mom said, "Dotty and Sally were inseparable, and both cut-ups. Got into all kinds of trouble together."

I snorted. "Those were the days of sock hops, poodle skirts and pony tails, right? Pretty demure times."

"Wrong decade. Dotty's high school and college days were the

’60s—the hippie era best known for free love, drugs and rock & roll.”

It was hard to remember Dotty hadn’t always pretended to live in 1910. She’d been an ordinary person until Thomas died. I tried to picture her as a young woman. “She was the flowers-in-your-hair type?”

“Wrong, again. Her hippie uniform was a green tee shirt, bell-bottom jeans and hoop earrings. In the parlor, there’s a picture of her back in the day.”

I didn’t tell my mother there were no pictures in the parlor. She’d find out later. “Okay, sounds like your itinerary’s set. How do I get Dad his medicine?”

“Leave it at the General Store with Kaitlyn. She’s the proprietor. We talked with her yesterday, and she seems really nice. We’ll swing by there at some point. Also, the cappuccino’s to die for. Don’t miss it.”

For supper, I ate the salad and lobster mac, which were delicious, and started feeling better. Maybe I had it wrong. Maybe something had come up to divert Dotty from her routine. I had to hope so, or I’d just curl up and cry again. With some effort, I shook off my dismal mood.

Then it was hard getting ready for bed at 9:00 pm, but 5:30 am would arrive all too soon. I thought of checking the remaining shelves in Thomas’ room for a book to lull me to sleep. His tastes had run to non-fiction, heavy on politics, history, science and archaeology. None of that seemed interesting. I preferred mystery, sci-fi, or romance. Correction: I used to read romance when I believed in it. Divorce crushes happily-ever-after fantasies.

Without something to occupy my thoughts, my room felt too large to be comfortable. It’d been designed for children’s sleep and play. With only a bed, night table, chest, and wardrobe, the space had an eerie emptiness. In fact, the whole house felt off in a way I couldn't put my finger on. Might just be Dotty's absence. Eventually, I slept.

I don't know what woke me, but as soon as my brain turned on, I heard noises downstairs. Wood scraped against wood. Crashes. Something fell and shattered.

My heartbeat pounded in my ears when I jumped up to lock my room. I struggled to control my breathing, to stay silent, ear pressed against the door. For some minutes, I heard nothing. Then, footsteps climbed the stairs.

I tiptoed to the chest under the window. *Please, please let the fire ladder still be there.* It was. Tugging on the window lifts produced no movement. *Aw, come on! Open, you damn thing*! I heaved. I heaved again. Finally, the strength of my fear shifted the sash enough to set the ladder and to squeeze myself through the opening. The climb down was fast; my sprint to Tyler's cottage faster.

Banging on his door, I waited, shivering in the wind. What if he were a heavy sleeper? I yelled, "Tyler! Get up. I need you."

A century or so later, Tyler opened the door. Blinking, he stared down at me. "S'up? This your idea of a booty call?"

Only then did I realize my thin cotton nightgown effectively concealed nothing. "No, you moron," I growled. My pointing finger shook along with my voice. "There! In the house…someone. Intruder. Burglar. A…a—"

"Slow down. What happened?"

"Noises. Furniture pulled or dragged. A crash. Footsteps on the stairs."

"Oh." Tyler waved off my words. "That's just Amanda."

"Who's Amanda?" I shrieked.

"Our ghost," he said levelly.

4.

I stood tapping my foot inside the door of Tyler's cottage. He'd pulled a jacket from a peg to put round me, then went off to get dressed. Though he was probably gone all of two minutes, when he returned in long-sleeved tee shirt and sweatpants, phone in hand, I was itching to get moving.

"Amanda was my 4th great-grandmother," Tyler began. "The original lady of the house. Her husband, Hiram, built it for his bride. He'd recently come into money, and so he decided to do the whole domestic thing: wife, kids, impressive home. Hiram was twice Amanda's age—"

"Skip the ghost stories, Tyler. I'm too old to be scared by them now, and we're wasting time. We have to catch the intruder! Keep him from robbing Dotty."

"No, we don't. The house is empty. No one's threatened. Dotty doesn't care about what's left in the place; everything she values is locked away, safe. And besides, there's a 99% chance of no robber. It's probably Amanda."

I wasn't buying this. "If you're too cowardly, I'll do it myself. I just need a weapon. Do you have a gun?"

"No." He looked around the room. "I have, uh, an old hockey stick and a fireplace poker. You choose."

"Okay!" I strode to the hearth, snatched up the poker and waved it like a sword.

Tyler burst out laughing. “You have no idea how silly you look. A woman who weighs…what? A hundred ten pounds soaking wet? Barefoot. In a nightgown and oversized jacket. Oh, you’re terrifying.”

I could feel blood rush to my face as I balled my free fist. I didn’t know whether to plead or to haul off and sock him. In the end, I did neither. Just stood there glaring.

“Sit down, Megan.” Tyler reached for the poker. “Let’s think this through.” I flounced onto his couch, still too furious for words. He set the poker back with the fireplace tools, and took a seat in an armchair. “First off, how could a burglar get to Spear Point? It’d be crazy to motor here in the dark with all the shoals, and a boat engine makes noise. Did you hear any motor sounds?”

“No,” I answered automatically, forgetting I didn’t want to talk to him.

“Neither did I, and I’m a light sleeper. Second, if an intruder—or intruders—could get here, they’d likely be armed. A poker and hockey stick are no match for guns. If we call the cops, they’ll have to wait till the tide recedes in three hours. In the meantime, what’s important is protecting ourselves.”

I wasn’t ready to concede. “What about Dotty’s pearls and cameos? Important papers—identity theft!”

“She keeps those in the Secret Room. Do you know how to get in?” He paused to nod at my head shake. “I don’t either, and I spent the better part of one teenaged summer trying to figure it out. The rest of her valuables are in the carriage shed.”

“The old shack? A hard sneeze could knock it down.”

“Not anymore. I tore off the walls and demoed the rest. Built an entirely new structure that’s waterproof and climate controlled. Glass block windows. Steel doors. Case-hardened locks.”

“You’re expecting World War III?”

"Flooding and hurricanes. We've had surges and King Tides like never before. One took out the planking on the dock all the way to the boat house. Couple of hurricane warnings, too. This cottage is low. I couldn't risk my work files and a few things I treasure to be swept away. Oh, and my car. Needed a place to keep it dry if we had to evacuate.

"I replaced the old walls so Dotty wouldn't have to look at a bunker. When the floors in her house sagged from too much weight, she had movers shift her collections to the shed. Discards were donated or went to Sam's antique store in town. So, you see," he concluded, "her prized possessions are secure."

"I thought Dotty liked clutter."

"Nah. She was stuck with it. What's still there she inherited from Thomas. He got the place from his first wife, Ellen, my grandmother, who kept it as she found it. According to Dotty, no one in all those generations pitched anything out."

"Well, that's odd," I said. "People always like to put their own stamp on their home."

"Dotty said she tried. When she was first married, she cleared the parlor and brought in her own furniture. At night, the banging and crashing downstairs kept the newlyweds awake. Thomas told her the Amanda story, mostly as a joke, but Dotty took it seriously. One night, she talked to Amanda, promising to bring back her possessions. Afterward, the house was quiet until Thomas built the Secret Room in the 1970s. The noises started up again. And now, with the house being revamped, I'm betting Amanda's back at it."

I shook my head. "Tyler, this is the kind of crap you told me when you didn't want me spying on you and your girlfriends."

"It is. I might have embellished a bit—added in gory details—but the basic story is true."

"So, what does this Amanda want other than to be a decorator?"

"My guess is she's looking for her children. She had three kids—bang, bang, bang—in four years. Then she died."

"Of what?"

"Probably having three kids in four years. Anyway, Hiram didn't know what to do with babies, so he took them to his spinster sisters in Brooklin—"

"New York?"

"Maine. Brooklin with an *i* not a *y*. It's five or six peninsulas northeast of here, best known as the area where the Viking coin was found. In fact—"

I cut into the history lesson. "Stick to the Amanda story."

"Right. There's not much more. Over the years, family members heard noises and footsteps going to the nursery. I don't know who first decided it was Amanda, but the story evolved into a search for her kids. As the theory goes, when something changes in the house, she gets confused and aggressive. She doesn't know where the children went or what became of them."

"What did become of them?"

"They grew up, came back to live with Hiram when they were adolescents, and went on to adult lives. The eldest, Harwood, was Hiram's heir. He continued the line—"

"That leads to your dad and you. Huh." I leaned on a hand, thinking about this. Tyler surely put a lot of money into the shed. He held title to the cottage. From the way he talked, he was pretty tight with Dotty, too. Did he expect to inherit Spear Point from her? The place had to be worth a lot, some millions, I guessed. Was he buttering up the old lady to get her property or…ohmygod, did he have something to do with her disappearance? Ice water ran through my veins.

"What?" Tyler asked, eyeing me closely.

"Nothing. I'm tired, and I still think somebody's lurking around here. What if he—or they— decide to hit this cottage next? Bust a window, force the door. Like you said, we have nothing much by way of defenses."

"We can go to the shed if you like. No one's getting in there."

I twisted my lips. Did I want to be holed up with Tyler in a bunker? Not tonight. "I have a better idea. I'm going to sneak down to the dock to see if there's a boat. If not, it's just us on Spear Point—and Amanda. She can have the nursery. I'll sleep in Dotty's room."

"Where's all this macho stuff coming from? You used to be scared of your own shadow. I called you Scaredy Cat, as I remember."

"Let's not play Twenty Questions. It's getting late." I rose from the couch.

"You'll cut your feet on the rocks, and I don't have shoes to fit you. I'll go." Tyler agreed with some reluctance, it seemed to me. He forced a smile. "I have more experience sneaking around Spear Point."

"True enough." Years ago, the tide made a good excuse for overnight revels with his teenaged posse. The boys couldn't get home, so they had to stay. After dark, they'd slip out to drink and smoke where they thought Dotty would be no wiser to their activities, but I knew what they were up to.

He waggled his eyebrows with false bravado. "Won't be long. Lock up after me." Before he left, he grabbed the poker.

I hugged his jacket tighter around me and hung onto the lapels as I rehashed the awful thought I had about Tyler. On TV detective shows, they say, "Follow the money" when they can't identify a villain. Money, in Dotty's case, led directly or indirectly to Tyler. If it wasn't for money, why had Tyler come to live on Spear Point? It'd be easier to stay in Portland where he worked.

There was his dad, John Hartley, to consider, too. John was Dotty's stepson. I hadn't heard anything about him lately other than he'd given his interest in the cottage to Tyler. Was John capable of hurting Dotty to enrich himself? Was Tyler? I only knew the vain kid from the past. I didn't know this adult Tyler.

I looked around the living room, trying to get a sense of the man. Décor was pure Maine cottage, comfy and inviting. Mostly blues and browns. No antiques, nothing valuable needing special care. The furniture was worn but intact. This was a place to kick back and chill.

Tyler wasn't a slob. The bathroom didn't disgust me. A peek into his bedroom showed no clothes on the floor, no tissues dropped after use. The kitchen sink was free of dirty dishes. Tyler's housekeeping moved him up a notch in my estimation.

I reflected on my ex, who thought the apartment was fine if he could wade through trash to the bed. Clean? Oh, my, no. It wasn't manly to clean.

My bitter thoughts and I went back to the couch to await Tyler. His environment could tell me only so much about him. How could I know what was in his mind? I'd have to stay alert and listen carefully to what he said.

When the doorknob twisted, I flinched, afraid it wasn't him until I heard, "Hey, Megan. Let me in." I opened the door, feeling an absurd sense of guilt, as though Tyler could know what I'd been thinking.

He gave me a thumbs-up victory salute. "Nothing there. Likely, it's just Amanda." After putting the fireplace poker in its holder, he said, "I could use a beer. Want one?"

"No. If we're lucky, we'll get a cat nap before it's time to leave for Hopewell. I'm going to the house."

"I'll come with you. Wait. Let me get some flashlights."

I didn't refuse this belated act of chivalry. Truth was, I dreaded entering the dark front hallway alone, and I welcomed a flashlight. The house didn't have overhead fixtures. All the lights were lamps, either standing or table. In some places, you had to walk through a whole dark room to get to a lamp. Old houses. Sheesh.

The moon was waxing, heading toward full, I guessed, so we had no trouble crossing the grass to the house without extra light. Tyler unlocked the front door, and there we were: inside. The hall lamp, affixed to the top of the newel post, was a statue of some half-clad nymph holding a yellow globe. It yielded about as much illumination as a night light. So, flashlights on, we sent our beams up the stairs and into the parlor. Nothing looked unusual.

"I'm going to check Dotty's room," I whispered. Hand reaching toward the doorknob, I faltered, arguing to Tyler, "If the ghost is angry about changes Dotty made, Amanda could be waiting to ambush Dotty in her bedroom. I really, really don't want to see a glowing-green specter hanging over me with some horrific expression on her face."

"Not a problem, Scaredy Cat." Tyler reached around me to turn the knob. "No one's ever seen Amanda. She doesn't manifest." He pushed the door open and stepped inside, making a show of peering beneath the bed with his flashlight before he turned on the bedside lamp. "No monsters hiding under the bed, either."

"You can stop now," I said sourly.

"Not till I check the bathroom." He did that and announced, "All clear."

We made our way through the parlor and dining room in silence. I planned to go to the kitchen first—I'd left the door to the screen porch open—but Tyler turned right, into the study.

We both shouted. My words were a little less crude than Tyler's, but my mother wouldn't like them. The place was a shambles. A lamp near the bookcases had fallen, it's glass shade shattered. The desk chair, made of solid wood with arms, had been shoved up against the nearest bookcase. Books were scattered on the floor, hanging off shelves, a few ended up on the desk and chair. Many of these were open, lying on their backs.

"Amanda must be on a rampage," Tyler said.

"This isn't ghostly work. Since when do ghosts stand on chairs to reach high places? Don't they just float or point their finger to move things like Patrick Swayze in *Ghost*?"

Tyler snorted. "You're asking me? How the hell should I know?"

"Someone was here," I insisted. "A real person. I think they were searching for something."

We both said, "The Secret Room!"

Tyler ran his hand along the groove between the two bookcases. Next, he tried to wedge in his fingers and pull the cases apart. "Won't budge." He huffed in frustration. "We have to leave this as it. Tomorrow, well, today, we'll bring in the cops. Let's finish going over the rest of the house."

In the kitchen, I had to swear again. Dotty's pie lay on the floor upside down. The thief—intruder, whatever—must have knocked it down, hopefully, on the way out. I knelt to clear the mess, but Tyler warned, "Don't touch it. Could have fingerprints."

I shot to my feet. Now feeling the anger and violation of a break-in, I locked the kitchen door, then the one in the laundry room. I was so fired up, I headed for the back stairs with no thought of ghosts. Tyler followed, and we inspected the upstairs rooms, including the nursery, which was just as I left it. After reclaiming the ladder and shutting the window, I grabbed phone and toiletry bag. I led the way downstairs. Even though the ghost story paled compared to the vandalism, I still wanted to sleep in Dotty's room.

"You'll be okay?" Tyler asked. "Staying here alone? You could crash on my couch."

"I'll be okay. I'll leave the bathroom light on. If you see it go off, come running."

"Will do. Are we still on for Hopewell in the morning?"

"Definitely. I need to deliver my dad's medicine, and we'll contact the police, right?"

"Have to pick up Dotty's bike from town hall, too. Yeah, good. I'll see you at 6:00." He nodded and went home. I locked up after him.

Before I approached Dotty's bedroom, I made a little speech to Amanda. Standing in the hall, I said, "Hey, Amanda. Um…hello. I'm Megan, just a visitor here while Dotty's away. I'm not going to do anything to your house, and I can't help you find your children. I'm really sorry about what happened to you. So, just let me sleep, okay? Please? Good night."

Was it my imagination or did the atmosphere in the house feel a little lighter? All I know is when I set the alarm on my phone and snuggled under the line-dried, sunshine-fresh quilt, I felt no fear. I fell into a deep, dreamless sleep.

5.

Hopewell Harbor nestled between two rocky peninsulas. The eastern one, tall enough to block the rising sun, was bathed in shadow, it docks deserted, as the fishing fleet had gone out for the day's catch. Only the bait shack, garlanded in multi-color lobster floats, rose to catch the glow of first light.

Across the harbor, pleasure craft in a marina rocked gently on dawn-glassy waves. One large ship was anchored out.

Pine and spruce blanketed the land, concealing meandering hiking trails. White and gray homes, each different, dotted the hillside.

A sliver of beach joined the twin arms of land. At this hour, only a lone jogger scared up squawking seagulls as he ran. Our road skirted the beach. We passed upscale shops offered art, antiques, hand-sewn accessories, sweets, and a food truck advertising lobster rolls. At the end of the street sat an old, white, steepled church.

Hopewell was perfect. Nearly. It had no police station.

"How can a town not have cops?" I asked Tyler.

"We're covered by the county sheriff's department with offices in Brunswick and Portland. So far, it's worked out."

"But what about emergencies?"

"The Fire and Rescue Station handles those."

"Violent crime?" I persisted.

Tyler drew back. "In *Hopewell*? Nah. Only problem with not having our own cops is the time it can take for response to nonemergency problems like our vandalism. Add in tidal blockage of Spear Point, and we could wait a while. Fortunately, we have an edge: Louise."

"Who's Louise?"

"Our all-knowing, all-powerful goddess a.k.a. the town clerk. If Louise wants a thing done, it's done. She's likely at the General Store having coffee now."

Tyler parked near the flat-faced General Store where, instead of tools and dry goods behind the plate-glass windows, we saw tables decorated with flowers. I stepped up toward the inset wooden screen door leading to the restaurant/grocery store. Shelves along the left wall held healthy foods of the non-GMO, organic, locally sourced free-range type. An alcove displayed local produce in wooden boxes, like an indoor farmer's market. Across the room a bakery nook tantalized me with the scents of cinnamon and fresh bread.

Early bird patrons included a man with a portable easel, a woman with double hiking poles, and a couple sipping coffee. Seeing them reminded me to order the cappuccino.

"Hey, Tyler," called a soprano voice. I turned to a young woman coifed in a red bandana putting set-ups on a nearby table. She came toward us. "Who's your friend?"

"My cousin, Megan Fields. Megan this is Kaitlyn Carter. She and her husband own the General Store."

"Oh, my parents said they enjoyed meeting you. They'll be here later today. May I leave some medicine for my dad with you? They may not make it to Spear Point before the tide shifts."

"Of course. Nice folks, your parents—and energetic. They made the rounds of nearly every place in town looking for info about Dotty."

"That's my mother, all right: Miss Energy." I pictured her running Dad ragged as he hid yawns behind his hand and yearned for his usual afternoon nap.

Kaitlyn frowned. “I am so, so sorry Dotty’s missing. Everybody in town adores her. Has there been any news?”

“Not yet,” Tyler said

“My parents are visiting an old friend of Dotty’s today. They’re hoping for a lead.”

“Good.” Kaitlyn smiled. “Have you come for breakfast or shopping?”

“Breakfast first,” I said.

Kaitlyn led us to a window table. I handed her the medicine package. “I’ll keep this by the register. Be right back with menus.”

I took a seat, but Tyler stood. “See the far table in back? Louise and Carla, town librarian, are there. I’ll have a word with them. Order me blueberry pancakes.”

“Want me to come?”

“I verk alone.” His attempt at an accent sounded more like Dracula than an action hero.

Kaitlyn returned with the menus, which I pretended to study. I already knew my order: two eggs over easy, rye toast and hash browns. My real attention was on Tyler as he approached the women to work his charm.

He used the same technique I’d seen him employ with teenaged girls: confident stride, friendly smile but head dipped a touch with false humility. The middle-aged women responded by halting what looked like an intense conversation. They sat straighter, and the one I guessed was Louise beckoned Tyler forward. It seems a handsome man is welcome no matter what your age.

Louise, in the power seat facing into the room, was a round brunette, smartly dressed in a navy collarless jacket, floral scarf and glittering jewelry. She had the placid assurance of someone used to receiving petitioners. To her left, now facing Tyler's seat across the table, was the librarian, Carla, a slight woman with fading blonde hair. All I could see of her clothing was a pink cotton sweater.

Louise spoke to Tyler before both of them turned their attention to the librarian, who displayed agitation and wrung her hands as she talked. Tyler listened with a concerned expression. I had to give the man credit: he knew how to exude sympathy and wait his turn.

When he did talk, both women were riveted by what he was saying until he paused, and then, Louise made her move. She reached for her phone, tapped in a number, and spoke a few words. Apparently not satisfied with the response, she spoke again with a severe expression on her face, and this time, she nodded. Clicking off, she told the others something to make them lean back in their chairs.

"Have you decided on your order?" Kaitlyn asked me.

I flinched. I'd been so focused on the rear table, I hadn't noticed Kaitlyn's arrival. I gave the order and went back to my gawking, but I missed the end of Tyler's performance, no doubt full of obsequious flattery and fulsome gratitude. When he left the ladies, his posture radiated triumph.

"Good news." He plunked down in the chair across from me. "Success. We're getting a detective at 4 p.m. today. Tide will be out, so he'll have plenty of time to investigate."

"A detective? Isn't that overkill for vandalism?"

"Not really. As it turns out, Hopewell's library was vandalized, too. Someone broke into the workroom in back and rummaged through boxes donated for the Labor Day used-book sale. Most of the boxes came from Dotty, Carla said. She'd been going through them slowly to make sure no rare books were in the lot. She didn't want to cheat Dotty."

"Well, that was kind of her," I said. "Did she find any?"

"No, but she did find a note—well, a love letter—from Thomas to Dotty. It was stashed in a book of poetry. Carla gave me the letter. She'd put it in her purse when she expected to see Dotty on Tuesday. Been carrying it around ever since." Tyler held up a white envelope.

"What's in it?"

I reached for the envelope but he snatched it away. "It's addressed to Dotty."

"So? Obviously, Carla read it."

"We'll find out when Dotty's back," Tyler said, "if she wants to tell us." He stood to stow the love letter in his back pocket.

"Pooh," I said. "Wait. Back up a bit. Why the detective?"

"Louise's idea. She thought Dotty's disappearance and two vandalisms connected to her couldn't be coincidence. The detective will visit Carla at 3:00 and us an hour later."

"Louise is right."

Tyler nodded, then looked up as Kaitlyn brought our breakfasts. We ate without talking, both intent on really good food and the puzzle of what these break-ins meant. At least, that's what I was thinking, and I assumed Tyler must be doing the same. When the food was done, I'd come to no conclusions. I told Tyler I wanted to buy some groceries. He asked for more coffee when Kaitlyn came by.

She said, "Oh, Tyler. I forgot to tell you a woman was in yesterday looking for you. Said her name was Chloe."

Tyler stiffened. "What did you tell her?"

Kaitlyn recoiled at his sharp tone. "Uh…I said I thought you were in Portland. Was that wrong?"

"No. Just right." Tyler' face turned stern, even grim. "If you see her again, say you don't know me well. I just show up once in a while on weekends—nothing more."

"Gotcha. This woman's trouble?"

Tyler blew air through his lips. "You have no idea." He shoved back his chair. "Forget the coffee. I better go tell Louise and Carla I wasn't here today and they don't know me, either."

When Tyler departed, I shared a curious look with Kaitlyn. She shrugged, and set down our bill. I followed her to the register to enter my card, all the while eying a cheese Danish calling my name. I paid cash for the sweet roll, and stood happily munching until Tyler rejoined me.

"No grocery shopping today." He took my elbow and steered me toward the door. "I'll make you dinner. You can shop tomorrow with your parents. They're staying at Spear Point tonight, right?"

"That's the plan, but—"

"Megan, we *have* to go."

I let him propel me through the door, but outside, I shook off his hand, planted my feet and insisted, "Tell me what's going on."

Tyler scanned up and down the street. "C'mon." He didn't quite run—it was more of a lope—but I scrambled to follow him to the car. When he clicked open the locks, I didn't touch the door.

"I'm leaving now," Tyler said firmly. "If you want to stay, you can hitch a ride with the detective." He got into the car and started the engine.

I sighed, opened my door, and plunked down on the seat. Tyler hung a U-turn and then drove out of town fast. He didn't speak or slacken the pace until we reached the road leading directly to Spear Point. There, among trees on both sides with only a few residences peeking through foliage, his breathing slowed and his hands lost their death-grip on the wheel.

"This woman," I said, "who is she?"

"Chloe Goode." Tyler snorted. "Goode! If ever there were a misnomer, that's it."

"She some throwaway one-night-stand you're dodging?"

Tyler turned to me, radiating disgust. "I don't know what you have against me, Megan, but I'm not the sonuvabitch you think I am."

Stung, and momentarily lost for words, I debated whether to apologize or go on the offensive. Offensive, it was. "This isn't about me. You're the one who's freaked out. Why?"

"It's not your business."

"Maybe it is. If this chick's gunning for you, I could be collateral damage."

Tyler hmphed. After a ruminative silence, he said, "All right. With Chloe lurking around Hopewell, you'd better know why I'm avoiding her. She's a stalker, delusional, convinced I'm her soulmate."

"So, an old girlfriend. This a fatal attraction kind of thing?"

He shook his head. "Never a girlfriend. I signed up for one of the online dating sites—"

"*You* did?" I balked at the idea someone with Tyler's looks needed dating help. Tyler Harley: 6'2", fit, dark hair, blue eyes. Yeah, his profile wouldn't draw much attention….

"Hey, I work all the time, mostly with men. I wasn't meeting any women. Chloe's picture looked good—blonde, nice face—so I asked her out for coffee at the shop across from my office. When I got there, she'd ordered me some nasty, sweet drink pretending to be coffee. I pretended to like it. She said, 'I knew you'd love what I love because we've been matched.' Our meeting went downhill from there. She talked about men only interested in her body and what she really wanted was a soulmate. 'And now I've found you,' she said, 'my soulmate!'"

"Uh oh," I said.

Tyler grimaced. "I thanked her for the coffee, headed to the office, and did some work before going home. Chloe called and texted a dozen times. I blocked the number."

"The next day, she showed up at my office, telling everyone she was my girlfriend and had to talk to me. I hustled her into the hall, told her not to come back, and I didn't want more dates. She said, 'Oh, but you will. We're matched—perfect for each other. You'll come around.'"

"How did she find your office?"

"Could be she followed me. My name's on the directory in the lobby, too. Anyway, not long after, Covid lockdown hit. I started seeing Nicole Seaver, a single mom who lived in my building. She'd been on my radar a long time, but you know how it is. We were always rushing off someplace, never had time to connect.

"During Covid, everything slowed down. We kept running into each other by the mailboxes, talked a bit, exchanged numbers, then called or texted at night. Some days, we'd meet at the park because her five-year-old, Molly, needed to play outside."

"Love in the time of Covid?"

Tyler smirked. "The good old days. So, things were going great until Nicole got a poison pen letter from Chloe. It said I was engaged to her. Chloe even added a picture of a left hand with ring."

"Oh, no! Did you tell Nicole Chloe was nuts?"

"I tried, but she was leery of me. I mean who'd expect someone to make up that story? Then Nicole caught Covid and needed help. When I delivered her groceries and medicine, she looks so ill, I stayed to look after her and Molly until Nicole was on her feet again."

"Didn't you get sick?"

"Yeah, I did. They took care of me. Thankfully, Molly never got Covid.

"By this time, I was serious about Nicole but she was focused on

Molly starting kindergarten. Molly was assigned to the afternoon session. When school let out it was kind of chaotic with kids, parents, teachers and cars all milling about. We finally found her, and saw the nametag sticker her teacher gave her had writing scrawled on it. It read Hello my name is Molly. *My mother is a whore.*"

"That's outrageous! What did you do?"

"Contacted the school, the police, and a lawyer to work up Protection Orders. The Orders weren't served because no one could find Chloe's address. The one she gave the dating service was bogus. She'd vanished, but Nicole didn't t stop worrying about Chloe. In the end, she left me, saying she had to protect Molly."

We'd reached the causeway to Spear Point. I felt sickened. I never thought I'd be sympathizing with Tyler, but here I was, angry and sad. I patted his arm. "I'm sorry," I said honestly.

"So am I." He heaved a hopeless shrug.

"Do you think Chloe's dangerous?"

"I don't know. Hard to tell what goes on in a twisted brain like hers."

After we bumped across the rocks to Spear Point, Tyler drove up to Dotty's door and parked. He looked at the house and then said, "Oh, damn. I totally spaced off picking up Dotty's bike. Too late now. The tide'll be rising before I'd get back. I'll have to call Big Rob in Public Works to see if he'll bring it over in his truck. Good for him to talk to the detective, too, since he found the bike in the cemetery."

"Police probably interviewed him already."

"Likely, but a detective might ferret out a small detail Rob didn't think was important."

I pictured Dotty putting fresh flowers on Thomas' grave. She wouldn't feel alarm if a young woman, a tourist, came up to her to asking for help with directions, a car problem, anything that might lure

Dotty to a waiting car. "Tyler, do you think Chloe could have kidnapped Dotty?"

Tyler swiveled in his seat to face me. "How would she know Dotty was related to me?"

"How did she know you moved from Portland to Hopewell?" I countered. "Chloe's obviously devious."

"But why Dotty? She's not a rival, not a threat to Chloe's romantic delusions."

"Not a threat, no, but a bargaining chip, perhaps. How long's it been since you last saw Chloe?"

He paused to think. "A while. Can't imagine why she hasn't found another target."

"I can. She took one look at you and decided she couldn't do better in a—" I made air quotes. "Soulmate."

"Oh, now, that's just…." He shook his head and waved away my words. "But Chloe might be trying to force me to deal with her. God," he moaned, "if she harms Dotty, it'll be my fault."

6.

Tyler looked stricken. He stared at me with haunted eyes and his face paled. Not even great actors could blanch on command. I knew, then, he wasn't involved in Dotty's disappearance, and I felt guilty about my suspicions last night.

I said, "This is all wild speculation. There's nothing to link Chloe to Dotty except our desperation to know where Dotty went."

He sighed. "But it's a possibility. I could have led that psycho here. I should have done more to find her, tell her face to face I didn't want her and never would."

I shook my head. "She wouldn't believe you. People like her only hear what they want to hear."

"I need to call the cops, at least," Tyler persisted, "to let them know Chloe's hanging around Hopewell."

"Problem is she's done nothing threatening here. There's no reason to detain her. If you have copies of the Protection Orders or statements you made in Portland, you should give those to the detective."

Tyler still looked bleak. To make amends, I said, "Come into the house. Let me get you a cold drink." Oops. All I had in stock was water and orange juice.

"Coffee." Tyler nodded. "I could use more coffee."

"Okay! Coffee, I have."

At front door, he handed me the key. "You should keep this."

"Thanks. Could come in handy."

We went through the house to the kitchen, where the first thing that caught my eye was Dotty's pie, still on the floor. It landed on a rag rug, saving the wood floor from blueberry stain, though the rug was destroyed. I looked at Tyler. "I'm itching to clean this up."

Eying the remains, he said, "The pie means Dotty planned to come back."

"I know. I figured that out yesterday."

"And you didn't say anything to me? Did you tell your parents?"

"Not yet. Mom still wants to believe Dotty chose to go somewhere."

I went to get the French press and the coffee canister, then filled the teapot from the bottled water dispenser. The heavy, glass bottle sat on a ceramic base with a spout. Our tap water came through an old pipe from the mainland. It was clean enough for washing but not drinking.

After switching on the electric stove, I set the kettle on it. As I spooned coffee into the French press, my phone buzzed. I answered and heard my mother's excited voice.

"Good news! We might have found Dotty."

"WHAT? How? Where? Wait. I want Tyler to hear, too." I turned up the volume and set the phone between us.

"You two getting along?" Mom asked.

"We're fine. Tell us!"

"Well, you know your father and I went to see Sally, Dotty's best friend from high school. She talked our ears off about the fun summer she and Bill, her husband now, had with Dotty and Fred, who was Dotty's boyfriend at the time—"

"News!" I demanded.

"Right, right. Last conversation Dotty had with Sally was about going back to Mt. Washington in New Hampshire. Dotty and Thomas honeymooned at the hotel in Bretton Woods. It's a big, old, historic place, just the type she likes. So, we called the desk, but they wouldn't give out guest information until we got the police involved. Then they said yes, a single woman checked in as Mrs. Hart."

"Hart, not Hartley," Tyler noted.

"Could be an input error. Anyway, she paid in advance in cash so no credit card data."

"Paying cash sounds like Dotty," I admitted, "but, surely, someone would have noticed her 1910-style clothing."

"They're having an *a cappella* music convention just now."

"What's that?"

"Group singing without musical instruments. Just voices. Think barbershop quartet. Lots of participants in costumes."

"Did you call her room?" Tyler asked.

"A number of times, but she didn't pick up, so we're on our way there now. It'll take a couple hours, but it'll be worth it when we find her."

Tyler pointed to the pie. I said, "Mom, Dotty baked a pie on Tuesday morning. We think she planned to come home to eat it."

"Dotty's impulsive. She married Thomas after knowing him for only two weeks. Either she forgot about the pie or abandoned it."

The kettle whistled. I poured water into the press as Tyler said to the phone, "I don't know how she could get to Mt. Washington."

"There's a train from Brunswick. She might have ridden into town with someone she knew, withdrawn money from the bank and caught the train." To my dad, Mom said, "Jason, pull over to that rest stop." Then, "Megan, Tyler, I've got to go. I'll call when we know something. Bye."

Tyler and I looked at each other. "You didn't tell her about the break-in here," he said.

"She didn't give me a chance. And, I'd like to talk to the detective first. Maybe there's been a rash of petty burglaries—a gang of kids going around breaking into places for kicks and giggles—you know, to be daring. Or maybe they're really out to steal."

"Kids? Why not adults?"

"What they did seems so random, so juvenile. Who trashes books? It's almost like they couldn't find anything valuable here or at the library, so they made a mess for spite."

I poured the coffee into pretty cups with pink flowers. "Milk? Sugar?"

"Black's fine."

We sipped strong, bitter brew. "I don't mind admitting it," Tyler said. "I'm confused."

"That's 'cause we have nothing to go on, no facts. Hopefully, we'll get some later from Mom or the detective. It's this waiting that's so hard."

When he finished, Tyler put his cup in the sink. "Normally, I'd do engineering work, but I've taken vacation days. Guess I'll get a little sun and air, go down to the grotto for a dip. Might clear my head. Want to come?"

Inside me, my teenaged self whooped. I slapped her silly. "No, I'll do a bit of research—can't stay unemployed forever—and then water Dotty's garden."

"Up to you." He turned to go, then stopped, facing me. "Oh, I changed the rainwater collection system for the garden. Water still flows through the gutters into the cistern, but you don't have to go to the cellar, turn on the pump and valve, then haul the hose outside through the bulkhead. I put in an outdoor tap and pump switch."

"I could kiss you!" Instantly, I regretted my words. Rattling on at top speed to cover my gaffe, I explained, "The cellar's always terrified me. When I was little, I was down there when the light bulb popped. I was sure a creature would come out of the cistern to eat me. Screamed my head off and ran for the door, but it'd locked behind me. Dotty got me out and put wax in the lock so I wouldn't get trapped again."

Tyler shook his head. "Scaredy Cat," he said gently. He smiled with his eyes and dimples. "You're sure you won't come to the grotto? It's better with company."

My teenaged heart flip-flopped. *Stop that!* "Maybe later," I lied.

Tyler left, and I went to tend the garden. Next, I retrieved my suitcase and carry-on from the nursery, bringing them down to Dotty's room. Curled up with my tablet in the nook window, I just got the answers I wanted and set my phone alarm before sea air and the rhythmic flow of waves lulled me to sleep.

Pachelbel's *Canon in D Major* woke me. Up and into the shower before the song finished, I turbaned my hair because there'd be no time to air dry. Then I put on the clothes I'd been wearing, opened Dotty's armoire, and checked myself in the door mirror.

Yuck. My tee shirt and jeans were baggy and looked like I'd slept in them, which I had. Detectives dressed pretty well, at least the ones on TV did. I thought of what was in my suitcase. I hadn't packed anything nice. As I recalled, Dotty was about my size.

A blouse caught my eye. It was fine white lawn fabric, had delicate cotton embroidery and, when I pulled it out to look closer, I saw tiny, perfect gathers forming full sleeves ending in lacy cuffs. Down the front ran a row of shell buttons, each with a satin button loop.

I imagined a cartoon devil on my left shoulder while an angel perched on my right. Devil: *Go ahead—wear it.* Angel: *You have no right to wear Dotty's clothes.* Devil: *Aw, just try it on.* Angel: *Don't you dare! Oof—* The angel's voice cut off when I flicked her from my shoulder.

I had barely enough time to put on the blouse, a long, navy skirt and sky-blue belt before the doorbell rang. Hastily adding a clip for a half up-half down hairstyle, I answered the door.

"Why are you dressed like Dotty?" Tyler demanded. Frowning, scrutinizing me, he stepped into the hall.

"I wanted to be presentable for the detective."

"You're dressing up for *him*?"

"Well, you did," I pointed out. Tyler wore a maroon dress shirt and chinos.

"This is work casual," he said. "You look like you're ready for a ladies' tea. The detective will think you did away with Dotty to steal her clothes."

The guilt that pulled back when I changed into Dotty's beautiful things slammed into me like a tsunami. My eyes welled up. Furious, ashamed, I wrenched open Dotty's bedroom door. I'd rather wear my rags than be called a thief—or worse.

Tyler followed me. I whirled on him. "Get out. I'm changing clothes."

"Don't…." He waved his hands. "Don't do that. Don't get upset. It was just a stupid joke."

"*Really* stupid," I spat out. "Now, where did I put—"

"Megan, stop. Please. I'm sorry. You look nice. Dotty would be tickled you like her clothes. How many women want to look like their great-aunt?"

I stood glaring at him, deciding whether to yell or cry. Surprisingly, I laughed.

The doorbell rang.

"Come along," Tyler held out his hand. "Come on, Megan."

I avoided touching him and went to the door. A man about Tyler's age with sandy blond hair stood waiting in sports jacket and slacks. He held a briefcase.

"Good afternoon. I'm Detective Erik Lundgren from the Sheriff's Department, here to see Tyler Hartley."

Tyler threw open the door. "Sonuvabitch! You?" He unceremoniously shoved past me to the porch. "Rik! Good God. Can't believe it."

Detective Lundgren and Tyler gripped and slapped in one of those sideways hugs men do. Then they gaped at each other until Lundgren said, "Thought I'd surprise you."

"You have. Jeez," Tyler said. "You swore you'd never be a cop like your dad."

"Yeah, well, times change. What's up with you these days?"

"Engineer. In Portland. Commute from here."

"Man, it's like a reunion. You know who else's in town? Colin Currie."

"They let him out of jail?"

Lundgren shook his head. "Never went to jail, just juvie. Guess it straightened him out. He's an ocean explorer now. Came in on the big ship moored in Hopewell Harbor."

"Treasure hunter," Tyler scoffed.

"'Bout sums it up," Lundgren agreed. "He thinks there's Viking artifacts somewhere around here. His crew's been hunting the nearby wrecks and islands."

"Good luck to him," Tyler sneered.

"But hey, now you're back, we should get together. Some of the guys still meet for poker and drinks—the ones who aren't married, anyway." Lundgren stared pointedly at me.

"This is Megan, my cousin. Megan Fields. She came up from Florida when Dotty went missing. Dotty's her great-aunt. Megan's staying here at the house."

Lundgren tilted his head. "You were that kid, the one who tagged after us, with the—" He tapped on his mouth.

"Braces."

"And pigtails!" He seemed delighted to remember that detail.

"One braid. It was the fashion. Now," I said shortly, "would you like to come in? Maybe investigate our vandalism?"

He shifted gears from bro to professional. It was almost comical to watch his shoulders pull back, his chin lift and his expression turn All Business. "Yes, thanks." He entered, and the three of us found seats in the front room.

"First off," I said, "I want to know if there's any news about Dotty."

"I wish there were. We canvassed the neighborhood, but nothing useful came of it. Still no ransom note?" He watched us shake our heads. "We have no leads. It's like she vanished into thin air."

"My parents think she might have traveled to Mt. Washington in New Hampshire."

"I heard something about that," Lundgren said. "Mrs. Fields called into the station about a woman at the big hotel. We asked the local force to check on the woman, but they had issues with reasonable cause and privacy." He sat back, saying, "Ty, tell me what happened here."

Tyler recounted the noises I'd heard and his checking the boathouse. He said nothing of Amanda, our ghost. I didn't blame him. He finished with the study vandalism and the overturned pie.

I asked if there'd been other burglaries in the area besides the library, but Lundgren said no. Summer, July in particular, was the high season in Hopewell. Summer residents and tourists left no unattended building as targets for theft. He noted everyone in town knew Dotty was missing and her home, presumably, empty, so our vandalism could have been a crime of opportunity.

Lundgren wanted to see the study next, so we headed to Thomas' room. "Hmm," he said, surveying the chaos. "Similar to the library. Books opened and scattered, as though they'd been searched. Looks like the intruders didn't make it into the Secret Room."

"Does *everybody* know about the Secret Room?" I grumbled.

"My old friends do," Tyler answered. "I told you I tried to get in when I was a boy. They helped me strategize."

"No joy there," Lundgren said. "The place is like a Chinese puzzle box. I wonder how Mrs. Hartley found the way in."

A thought started to form in my head. It grew and grew as Tyler led the detective into the kitchen to inspect the pie.

Lundgren opened his case, took out gloves and a plastic bag. "Damn shame. Mrs. Hartley makes sensational pies. I'll collect the pan for evidence, maybe get fingerprints, but it's likely no one touched it besides her. Looks like it fell when someone passed by. I'll take a few books from the study, too. Problem with books, though, is they have all kinds of prints."

"Tyler," I said slowly, "the envelope the librarian gave you. Do you have it in your pocket?"

"Nope. It's in my jeans."

"Maybe you should get it. If these break-ins are related, people are looking for something in a book. That note was in a book."

"But it's a love letter, only important to Dotty."

"Love letter?" Lundgren asked.

"From my grandfather. Dotty probably used it as a bookmark."

A car horn honked. "That'll be Big Rob with Dotty's bike," Tyler said. "You should talk to him since he found the bike at the cemetery."

"He was interviewed, but it wouldn't hurt to ask a few more questions." Lundgren turned to me, "Miss…er, Mrs.—"

"Ms.will do."

"Ms. Fields, thanks for your time. Just one thing more: Were all the house doors and windows secured?"

"No. I forgot to lock the laundry room door."

He nodded. "I'll check outside for signs of breakage, but there's the probable entrance. I'll dust for prints. Be sure to lock up tonight."

"I will. Thank you for coming, Detective Lundgren."

"It's Erik. We're not real formal around here." He reached into his jacket pocket to hand me his card. "Call or text if you need to talk to me." Then he stood back for a moment, inspecting me, before saying, "I should have known you were kin to Mrs. Hartley. She's a special lady. You resemble her."

The comment surprised me, but I liked being compared to Dotty, so I smiled. After revisiting the study, the men left. I eyed the blueberry mess and nearly bent to start cleaning before I caught myself. *Not in Dotty's clothes!* Off to the bedroom I went to fetch my old clothes, feeling like Cinderella after the ball.

7.

By the time I finished cleaning up blueberries, Tyler hadn't returned. I poured myself a glass of juice and waited. When he came in, he said, "Big Rob remembered being late to mow the grass in the cemetery because of a car club parade going through Hopewell. Bunch of rich dudes from Brunswick with their oh-so-special cars on their way to Portland."

"Could one of them have taken Dotty?"

Tyler rolled his eyes. "Think about it: A driver halts, stops the parade. 'Hey, guys. Just gonna snatch that old woman there and throw her in the trunk. Won't take long.'"

"Okay," I conceded, "but someone else might have used the commotion to grab Dotty."

"We're back to Chloe, aren't we? I told Rik about the harassment in Portland and showed him copies of the paperwork. He said I'd need to file a new complaint, so I called my lawyer, who'll overnight forms to my P.O. box in Hopewell.

"Rik also said he'd follow up with the car club, and tell the cops who patrol Hopewell to keep watch for Chloe. He seemed happy to have something concrete to do at last."

"Good," I said. "Must be hard to be a detective with nothing to detect."

"He asked about you," Tyler said. "Wondered if you were seeing anyone. Thought he'd ask you to dinner. I said you didn't have time."

"You took it upon yourself to answer for me?"

Tyler waved an airy hand. "Rik's a player. You don't want to get mixed up with him."

"I make my own decisions, Tyler Hartley." I stomped out, heading to the bedroom where I'd left Erik's card. I pulled out my phone, then set it aside. Didn't want to look too eager.

When I returned to the kitchen, Mr. Know-It-All was gone. Good riddance. I could start on supper, I supposed, though this morning, Tyler offered to cook. I'd had enough of his arrogance for one day; better to eat alone. But the sun wouldn't set for another two to three hours. A dip in the grotto could fill the time. Tyler had already been there, so he wouldn't bother me.

Ten minutes later in suit and tee shirt, carrying a beach towel, I reached our ole swimmin' hole, which was, in fact, a hole. Some lady of the house in the old days disliked sea life, waves and cold water. Her indulgent husband converted a natural inlet to a bowl carved into the rocks. Workmen piled the excavated stone around the pool's edge to make an enclosure roughly twenty feet in diameter open to the sky so sunlight could warm the shallow water.

It was a nice, calm space. So nice, harbor seals moved in, frightening the dainty lady.

Back came the workmen to raise the walls, cantilevering slabs inward to block the seals. They did a good job; those stones stayed in place, creating what we called a grotto, though it remained roofless.

I went down the steps, surprised to see solar lamps. Tyler's idea, surely. The sun was in the west, so the east side of the grotto was light. On the west side, a lamp glowed.

Even on the light side, the water would be chilly. It should warm by August, but this was July. My only choice was to suffer piecemeal or all at once. I picked bit by bit, dunking toes, then legs, then sitting down in water no deeper than a soaking tub, but yikes! I gasped when the cold hit my core.

Behind me, I heard, "You made it. How's the water?"

Tyler. "Fine," I lied without facing him. "Thought you'd been here today."

"Nah. Sacked out instead. Hardly got any sleep last night."

Tyler went to the spot we use as a slide. It's just smoothed rock that slants into the water with all the vertical drop of a kiddy pool, but it's slippery. He used it to submerge. When he popped up, he tossed his hair, then squeegeed with both hands. Dripping wet, he looked like a men's cologne ad. "You're right. Water's great. Toasty, even."

I flashed an evil grin.

He moved nearer, to a place where he could stretch out both arms and lean his head against the ledge. "So, you going out with Erik?"

"Haven't called him yet."

"Don't say I didn't warn you about him."

"Are you saying he's dangerous?"

"Rik? No. Just gets distracted by every hottie he sees. Used to be a heartbreaker back in the day."

Eyes narrowed, I said, "Since when do you worry about my feelings? The summer we were both here, you treated me like dirt. I was lonely, Tyler. I wanted kids to talk to. You had friends, but every time I got near your entourage, you'd say, 'Go play somewhere else.' Play! Like I was five years old. I was *thirteen*."

"You looked younger. No makeup, and those little, frilly, uh—"

"Sundresses. I thought the ruffles would hide my flat chest."

Tyler's eyes slid in for an update, but the part he sought was under water. I said, "For the record, my chest's not flat anymore."

He looked away while I pressed on. "I tried to do makeup, but I botched the job. It's my coloring. Everything on my face is pale. Red eyebrows, blonde lashes, blue eyes that look gray most of the time. Ring my lids with dark lines, and I could pass for a vampire. Bright lipstick? I'm a clown."

Turning to me, he said, "You look good now."

I cast my eyes heavenward and lifted a hand to my cheek. "Be still, my beating heart. Second compliment in one day!"

Exasperated, Tyler argued, "No matter what I say about you, you throw shade at me. Why?"

Ready or not, it was time for the truth. "Because…because you ignored me when I was desperate for your attention. I had a world-class, teenaged crush on you."

"Me?"

"You were popular and handsome. What else could a thirteen-year-old girl want?"

"Hmm. And now?"

Was he questioning my feelings or plans? I'd answer both. "I want more than a pretty face."

Tyler sank into the water up to his neck, asking, "What's the name of the guy you married?"

"Chase."

"Figures." He smirked.

"There wasn't another woman, if that's what you mean."

"No? Always thought there had to be another woman—or man. Never can tell, these days."

"Not this time," I said. "We stopped seeing life the same way. At first, we agreed to work our way up, you know, a small apartment to a bigger one or a house, starter jobs to better ones, have kids when the time was right.

"Then Chase found a niche he liked, and wanted to stay there forever, never change. He had a dead-end job, but refused a really good offer. 'Too much work.' Buy a house? 'Too much work.' Kids? Same."

"What was he saving himself for?"

"Video games. He lived for those stupid games. On date nights, he'd hand me a beer and a spare controller."

Tyler pursed his lips and stayed silent a moment before saying, "My parents split up over a woman—Michelle, my former high school classmate. We called her Mickey Mouth."

"To her face?"

"It's not what you think. She used to flame her cast-off boyfriends on social media. Her cruelty was funny, got a lot of likes. I steered clear of her, and a good thing, as it turns out. Awkward to have your stepmother be an ex. They have a kid now, Eliot. Calls me Uncle Ty."

"But you're his half-brother not his uncle."

"When he was little, Mickey thought it'd confuse him to have an adult brother. It's ironic." Tyler huffed mirthlessly. "As an only, I always wanted a brother. Be careful what you wish for."

I nodded. "How's your mom?"

"Broken. It's been eight years, but she still rages about him. We don't talk often. Dotty was furious at the way Dad treated my mom. She disowned him, refuses even to mention his name. Dotty's pretty much my only family now. Damn it! We have to find her."

"We will."

"But how? It feels so wrong to be lounging here when she's missing. Maybe someone's hurting her. Maybe she's terrified, panicked, nearly out of her mind. Maybe she's dead."

"My dad always says don't give up until there's no hope. She could have done what my mother said—gotten a ride to Brunswick, gone to the bank, and taken the train."

"Everyone in Hopewell knows she disappeared. Why wouldn't

this ride-giving friend come forward?"

I had to think about that one. "What if…what if the driver didn't return to Hopewell? What if he or she went north for, say, a hiking trip? Unplugged, not getting news, a person wouldn't know to inform the police."

"No phone? Be crazy to hike that way."

"People do it all the time. They go into a forest or desert or the mountains, get lost and have to be rescued. Even with a phone, there can be no service or a dead battery. It's a thin hope, I know, but it *is* hope. Let's hang onto it."

Tyler gave me a lip shrug. "At least, we haven't had bad news." He reached for his towel. "Thought this place would revive me, but I'm just cold and hungry. You okay with burgers?"

I reconsidered my plan to eat alone. No point in being surly. After my Big Confession, which wasn't such a big deal after all, I felt lighter, freed. I didn't need Tyler's approval, then or now. "Sure. There are veggies in the garden—couple of tomatoes and some small, green onions."

"I like the big Bermudas," Tyler said. "Dotty keeps those in the cellar."

"Uh…."

"I'll go down and get them after I change. Oh, and I hope you like sesame seeds. I have great buns."

I shut my eyes and fought to stifle my giggle. Half a dozen bun jokes came to mind. Finally, laughter won.

He caught on, groaned, and said, "You're being adolescent."

"I know," I gasped out. The laughter just wouldn't stop.

Tyler picked up his towel, wrapped it around his waist, and marched up the rock stairs with exaggerated dignity.

I yelled, "Ty, wait up!"

He stopped. "It's Ty, now? We're friends?"

"We're getting there." I grabbed my shirt and draped the towel over me like a cape. As we walked toward the houses, giggle fits overtook me, bubbling up unbidden until Tyler gave me a back-handed wave off and marched away to his cottage.

I showered to shed the salt, treated myself to clean, rumpled clothes from my suitcase, and then called Erik. After some chitchat, he asked me to dinner on Monday, his day off. He'd pick me up in his boat, we'd cruise a while, then eat seafood at "this little place on the big island. Sensational food. We'll have to return to Spear Point before the tide shifts, or my boat'll scrape bottom in your boathouse." Nothing he said raised any sense of alarm in me, despite Tyler's dire warnings. I told Erik I looked forward to Monday because I did.

Next, I called my parents. I hadn't heard from them, so I worried something was wrong. Oddly enough, I was right. Their car overheated; they had to pull into a local garage for a hose replacement. Lots of paperwork because the car was a rental. At long last, they were nearing Bretton Woods. Mom said she'd call me later.

The doorbell rang. I asked through the closed door, "Who's there?"

A disgruntled Tyler answered, "Me, of course. You expecting someone else?"

"Just being cautious." I let him in and stared blankly at him. "Am I late? Was I supposed to rush right over?"

"Onions. In the cellar. You wanted me to get them."

"Oh. Yes. Of course." My words came out stilted, as though I were lady of the manor and he a mere worker on the estate. Here I was, being territorial, though I'd only been in the house a little over one day. Tyler gave me an irritated side-eye, then led off toward the laundry room and its door to the cellar.

The door was old and worn. It wasn't in the swanky part of the house, so no one paid much attention to it. It needed paint, and the lock was one of those boxy things with a little knob on the front to control the bolt. The knob was glazed with the ancient wax Dotty used to keep it from locking all those years ago. I touched it, and felt closer to her, if only for a moment.

Tyler twisted the doorknob and pushed, but the door only moved inward an inch or so. He looked puzzled. "What the hell? It's stuck. It was fine last time I checked the cistern."

"When was that?" I asked.

"Couple weeks ago," Tyler answered absently. He pushed harder on the door. When nothing happened, he shoved with his shoulder with no result.

He stood back, scrutinizing the door. "Must have warped, like so many doors and windows in the house. Thought this one was all right. It's never acted up before."

"Could ghostly Amanda be pranking us?" I teased.

"I don't see her as a handyman." Tyler pressed all around the frame, kneeling to feel the low parts. "Here," he said. "It's sticking between the bottom and hinges. I need a light." He felt his back pocket. "Damn. Left my phone on the charger. Didn't think I'd be here long. Where's yours?"

"In the bedroom."

"Never mind. Get me the flashlight—two drawers left of the silverware. And a screwdriver. Big one. Same drawer."

I snapped to attention. "Yes, sir!"

"Please," he added.

After rooting through the drawer, I found what he wanted. "How old is this flashlight?" I asked, eying the brass tube with its bulging lens and ball knob switch.

"1918." Tyler took the light from my hand. "I asked Dotty about it once. Hope the batteries are still good. I don't know when they were last replaced."

"They had batteries in 1918?"

"Yep." Tyler stretched out on his stomach, setting the light on the floor so it would shine beneath the door. "There it is. Screwdriver." He shifted enough to hold up his hand.

I slapped it into his palm like a surgical nurse assisting a doctor. Tyler started probing, wiggling the screwdriver, and finally pounding the end with his fist. We heard a thump-thump-thump as something bounced down the stairs.

"Gotcha!" Tyler said to the door. This time, when he pressed, the door opened.

"Turn on the stair light," I urged. I did not like the darkness staring at me.

"Wait a minute. I saw something in the dust." He picked up the flashlight and trained it on the steps. "Would you look at that!"

"What?" Snake, rat, mouse—monster?

"It's a footprint."

"Oh," I said. Then, "Oh!" He handed me the flashlight. I bent over it to peer below.

"I see more of them, up and down the stairs. Look there." Tyler turned to me. He recoiled, crying, "Uck! What's wrong with your eyes? They're *white*!"

I moved the flashlight away from my face. "Better now?"

"Yes," he said, exhaling noisily. "Why did your eyes go all wonky?"

"It's only reflection, like glare. They're such light blue, sometimes they look white or even silver. Takes just the right angle and amount of light."

"Like from a 1918 flashlight. You shocked hell out of me."

"Now who's the Scaredy Cat?"

Tyler returned his attention to the stairs. "The prints are small, at least, smaller than my feet."

"Dotty?"

"She wears shoes with little heels not boots with deep lug soles. No, this was someone else. I'm going down."

I caught his arm. "If you step on the prints, you'll smear them. I'll get my phone. We need photos—and better light, too. Flip the wall switch."

Under bright light, the prints disappeared, the contrast between dust and footsteps too faint. We had to use the flashlight. Luckily, my phone could cope with dimness. After I brought it in, Tyler took shots from above, then said, "Gotta check this out."

Moving slowly and carefully along the edge of the stairs, he kept well away from the footprints. At the bottom, he yelled up to me, "I found a wooden shim pushed under the door."

I called, "Where'd it come from?"

"Me. I left a pile of wedges down here after I was done leveling furniture."

Okay, I was scared of the cellar, but my curiosity couldn't wait for Tyler's reporting, and he was down there. I wouldn't be alone. I stepped where he had stepped on the stairs, meeting him at the bottom. He said, "Footprints all over the place—around the cistern, along the shelves where I put my shims. The intruder used one to shove under the door."

"But why? And who?"

"My guess is last night's vandal. We must have surprised him when we checked the house. He had to find a hidey hole, and figured the cellar was best. Made sure we couldn't open the door."

"We didn't try." I shook my head. "We ignored the cellar."

"Lucky for him. Anyway, once things got quiet, he nipped out the bulkhead. It locks from inside. All he had to do was slide the bolt." Tyler opened one bulkhead door to twilit sky, and stepped up to garden level. In a short time, he was back, saying, "Nothing to see. Ground's too hard for tracks." He locked the doors and said, "Tomorrow, I'm chaining the bulkhead closed."

"Let's call Erik. We can send the pictures. For now, I've seen enough; that is, if you're sure no one's here." I eyed the cistern.

Tyler lifted the wooden cover. "Unless he breathes water, he's gone."

We went up to the laundry room, then to the kitchen, and sat at the table staring at each other until I asked, "What if the guy didn't leave last night? What if he waited for us to go to Hopewell this morning—and I spent the night here alone with a criminal!" I shuddered. "Ty, does your offer of the couch in your cottage still hold?"

"Sure. But, uh, you should get the bed since you're—"

"A woman?"

"I was going to say a guest."

"Tell you what," I posed, "we'll flip a coin for it."

Tyler smiled. "Deal."

8.

The sunset was a spectacular cocktail of orange, cherry, and lemon light. Tyler and I sat at a picnic table outside his cottage eating perfectly grilled cheeseburgers—minus tomato and onion. We'd completely spaced picking garden veggies after finding the footprints.

"You really do have great buns," I said.

"Don't start," Tyler warned as he adjusted the camp lantern's brightness.

"No, I mean it. These taste freshly baked, not like the ones in a bag with so many preservatives they'll probably last until the end of the world."

Tyler raised an eyebrow. "You think The End is Near?"

"With the current political situation, I'd say it's 50-50."

"You're a pessimist."

"Only when justified," I assured him. Then my phone buzzed. Somehow, I knew it would be bad news.

Mom's voice was subdued. "Dotty's not here. Mrs. Hart is a nice lady who was sympathetic when we approached her. She has hearing loss and a caption phone. Anyone she wanted to talk to knew that, so she didn't answer the room phone. She's waiting for her children and grandchildren to arrive. They're having a family reunion of sorts."

I heard the catch in her voice—the choked-back sob. "Aw, Mom. I'm so sorry."

"We failed! After all this running around, we're not one inch closer to finding Dotty. I'm heartsick. Your father's exhausted from driving. We're staying here for a day or two to rest up."

Tyler mouthed 'car parade'.

"We saw a detective, Mom, and he said there'd been a car club parade through Hopewell the morning Dotty went missing. They drove by the cemetery. The detective is interviewing participants."

"Oh, that's good. Maybe one of them saw something." She paused, then asked, "Everything okay there at Spear Point?"

"Here? Uh...." Tyler waved both hands at me. I understood. "All's well."

Mom yawned. "I'm bushed, going to bed, so I'll say goodnight. Love you."

"Love you, too. Hug Dad for me."

When I clicked off, Tyler said, "Wrong time to tell them about our intruder."

"I know. I just hate lying to her."

Tyler offered a beer from the cooler. I declined." Beer reminds me of Chase."

"I have a bottle of wine inside. Been keeping it for Dotty's birthday in September. It's Australian shiraz, her favorite."

"Mine, too," I said.

"Then I'll get it." While Tyler went to fetch the wine, I picked at my salad. It was the pre-made kind, unremarkable, so different from the flavorful ones Dotty made with fresh leaf lettuce from her garden. I rubbed my face, wishing I could scrub away my anxiety.

Tyler returned with the bottle, a corkscrew, and two empty jelly jars. "Don't have fancy glassware." He poured garnet streams of wine into the humble containers.

I raised my jar. "To Dotty."

Tyler clinked with me. "So, now what do we do for hope?"

"Hope Erik gets info from car club members." I took the first delicious sip, sighed, then sipped some more. "I noticed, when you talked to him about the footsteps, you used the word *he*. It could be a she."

"Chloe in hiking boots?" Tyler crossed his arms and gazed up toward the darkening sky. "Nah." He returned his focus to me. "She didn't strike me as the lumberjack type."

"Let's hope she hasn't taken up chainsaw log-cutting competition as a hobby," I quipped. I twisted my lips as a thought hit me. "You've never told me what she looks like."

Tyler frowned. "Uh, well, she's pretty, I guess. Leastways, I thought so when I saw her picture—before I knew her. Good body."

"Hair color? Eyes? Height?" I prompted.

"Blonde. Looked natural."

I snorted. "Men always think blonde hair is natural. But go on."

"Eyes…brown. She's about your height."

"So, 5'6"-5'7"." I set down my wine. "I wear size nine shoes. Do you think the tracks are nines?"

"I don't know women's sizes. I'd say an eight or nine men's, but the forensic guy should tell us for sure. Rik will show him the photos tomorrow. He didn't think they'd need impressions from the stairs because the photos were clear."

Tyler drew back from the table. "Enough speculation; enough running in place. New topic," he decreed. "I've been thinking about what you said today, how you were lonely here as a kid. You wouldn't have fit in with the guys—we were a pack of horny wolves back then—but I could've introduced you to the girls."

"I hated those girls," I said, watching him refill my jar. "I envied them because you liked them but not me."

"You were really that into me?"

I lifted my hand, sweeping right to create an imaginary celestial banner. “Tyler Hartley: Sun. Moon. Stars.”

“Jeez. I had no idea. You were a kid, a snitch and a cousin.”

“I only tattled once, the night you got drunk and decided to dance on the rocks. I was terrified you’d fall in and drown.”

“Dotty grounded me for a month,” Tyler recalled.

“And you never tried that again, did you?” I said smugly. “But let’s get one thing straight: We are *not* cousins. We share zero genes. You’re Thomas’ line with his first wife, Ellen. I’m Dotty’s line through her sister, Julie. We’re only connected by marriage.”

“So, what should I call you?”

“Dotty’s great-niece. Or friend.” I stood, stepped over the bench, and reseated myself facing the ocean. “The stars here are so amazing, even with a full moon.”

Behind me, I heard Tyler clearing the table. “Should I help?” I asked over my shoulder.

“Not much to do. Enjoy your stargazing.”

I took him up on that after reclaiming my wine. The air was balmy, with just enough breeze to be refreshing. Flashes from lights set at the end of peninsulas passed by. Waves and a lone seagull cry were the only sounds.

Tyler came back and sat beside me on the bench. “It’s so nice there aren’t mosquitos,” I said. “Why not?”

“No standing groundwater—fresh, that is. Mosquitos can’t live in salt water.”

I made a toast. “Here’s to salt water!”

“Think you’ve had enough wine?” He reached for my jar.

I held onto it, draining the last drop. “*Now*, I’ve had enough.” Ready to go inside, I carried the jars and bottle while Tyler picked up lantern and cooler. I stopped to look toward the causeway. “Tyler, could someone swim or row to Spear Point when it's an island?"

"Not if he wanted to live. Current's wicked fast because the gap between mainland and island is narrow. Depending on which side of the causeway a swimmer or rower picked, he'd be slammed onto rocks or launched toward open water where sharks could get him."

"We have sharks? Not those big ones from the movies."

"Yeah, those. Great whites. They're moving north because coastal waters are warming. Used to hang around Massachusetts, but now they've reached Maine. A woman died from shark attack near here a couple years ago. First-ever shark death in Maine."

We weren't even close to the water's edge, but I wanted to be inside. Immediately. When the cottage door shut behind me, I breathed easier. I set jars and wine by the sink.

A mound of bedding on the couch confronted me. I'd lost the coin toss, so the couch would be mine tonight. Tyler teased me when I walked out of Dotty's bedroom with an armload of linens. "Sure you don't need a porter?" I told him I was minimizing his housework: no sheets to wash when I was gone. He didn't make any other smart remarks.

"It's not late," he said, after consulting a tide chart on the wall, "but tomorrow's another early morning for me. Low tide's at 4:49 a.m. I should leave around 6:00. I have to visit the post office to pick up papers my lawyer sent. You don't need to come. You could sleep in."

"And miss those fabulous cinnamon rolls? No way."

He nodded. "You could do some grocery shopping if you want."

"What about Chloe? What happens if she's there and sees you?"

Tyler shifted his feet, taking a wider stance as though bracing himself for combat. His eyes narrowed, but his voice was even. "I'm ready for her now, sick of playing defense. I'll tell her to go to hell, leave me alone. But what I really want is to confront her about Dotty—watch her face, see if she shows any sign of awareness or fear."

"I like that idea." If she appeared when I was with him, I'd watch her body language closely, too.

"You have what you need?" Tyler asked.

I pointed to the mound.

"Silly question." He left for the bathroom.

I laid out sheets and pillows, then set my towel, toiletry bag and phone on the coffee table. Something was missing.

When Tyler reappeared, wearing only blue boxers, he said, "This is how I sleep. Am I supposed to cover up for you?"

"I've seen men in underwear before. I won't have to avert my maidenly eyes. What I do need from you is a blanket. I forgot to bring one."

"You can have my quilt. I'm always hot in bed."

"Really," I said, striving for wide-eyed innocence.

He grimaced. "Is this the way you are all the time, or do I bring out the worst in you?"

"Bit of both. You set yourself up so brilliantly." I gave in to a laugh—just a tiny one.

Tyler brought in the quilt and heaved it at me. "I'm racking it. Good night." He shut his door with more vigor than necessary.

In the bathroom, I found his jeans on the floor. When I picked them up to hang on the door hook, a white envelope fell from the pocket. I didn't give the devil-angel duo time to assemble on my shoulders. I pulled Thomas' letter from its envelope, sat on the tub edge, took the letter from the envelope, and read.

Beloved,

Your touch warms my heart. Your love lifts the crosses I bear.

You are my anchor through life's stormy seas and the rose that makes everywhere a garden. You are the key to my happiness, my treasure.

Thomas

I was disappointed. Though I had to give Thomas props for passion, the expressions were cliché. Any smitten high schooler could have come up with the symbols he used—heart, cross, anchor, rose, key, treasure.

Thomas had been a diplomat: Weren't they supposed to be good with words, persuasion, nuance? Of course, my dad always said *diplomat* was a euphemism for *spy*. What were spies good at?

Duh.

I bounded to Tyler's room. "Tyler! Ty! I've found something."

He threw open his door, scanning left and right. "Intruder? What did you see?"

"Nothing." I waved the letter at him. "This isn't about love. It's code. Thomas was telling Dotty how to get into the Secret Room."

Tyler snatched the letter from my hand, read it, and shook his head. "How's this supposed to work?"

"I don't know, but I remember those symbols from the bookcases. The two cases on the west wall had a heart between them. South wall, with three cases, had two symbols: cross and anchor. East wall has a rose. The Secret Room is behind the east bookcases because there are no windows on the outside wall."

Tyler looked dubious. I told him, "I used to hunt for something to read in Thomas' room. His library was dull, but now and then, I'd find a good book like the one that explained symbols in art."

"You read it," Tyler said flatly.

"Of course, wouldn't you?"

"Not my first choice."

"Well, I told you I was lonely. Didn't say how bored I was. I'd just started liking art, and the book had pictures. When I noticed the symbols on the bookcases, I looked them up. Heart, cross, anchor, and rose are Christian symbols. I imagined them carved into the cases by devout cabinetmakers. I felt safe in the study, even though the rest of the house creeped me out with all the gargoyles and weirdities Dotty used to have."

"She didn't have gargoyles."

"You know what I mean. The point is Thomas was writing instructions not poetry."

Tyler handed me the letter. "I saw those carvings, too. I pushed, pulled, twisted and tried to slide them all. Nothing happened."

"You didn't know the right order. And—"

"Neither do we," Tyler said. "Besides, only the east-wall bookcases are still in the house. The others are at Sam's antique store in Hopewell. Even if we figure out which symbols to use, they're not here. Let's sit down and think about this."

We went to the living room, where I plunked onto my makeshift bed. Tyler disappeared into his bedroom a minute and came back wearing sweatpants and tee shirt. I guess modesty prevailed with him after all.

"So," he said, taking a seat in the armchair, "Thomas left Dotty instructions. But those symbols are at the top of the cases, near the ceiling. I won't believe Thomas moved a ladder around from wall to wall to enter a room he designed. It'd take too long and be a lot of work.

"And there's another thing," Tyler went on. "Dotty let five bookcases go. If she needed them to enter the room, she'd have kept them, even though they were weighing down the house."

I had no answers to those objections. Instead, I'd been focusing on something else. "There are other words: *garden*, *key*, *treasure*."

"No way. I won't dig up Dotty's garden," Tyler declared. "She would kill me. And I could excavate the whole thing but still miss something small like a key. Besides, none of this matters. We're looking for Dotty, not some treasure."

I knew, then, what had been nagging at me since the librarian gave Tyler the letter. "I think Dotty's disappearance has to do with treasure. Someone searched her house and the books she gave to the library. Whatever that person wanted was in a book. This letter is it."

Tyler sat forward in his chair. "There'd have to be at least two people to be in both places the same night. The joke's on them. There's nothing in the Secret Room besides old furniture and what Dotty put there."

"What? How do you know?"

"A while ago, my dad told me what went down after his father was car bombed. Dad and Mom came here for Thomas' funeral. I guess I was here, too, but I don't remember. I was only two when he died.

"Dad said men from the government informed Dotty they'd be taking Thomas' diplomatic papers. Before they arrived, my dad sneaked inside the Secret Room. Dotty must have figured out how to open it. Dad saw a wall of guns, file cabinets, and a desk with passports and foreign currencies. He didn't have time to look any further because the men arrived and booted him out."

"Ah ha!" I cried. "So my father learned the story of Thomas the Spy from your dad. I thought it was just a rumor."

Tyler wasn't listening. He was looking up and away. "Colin Currie. He's a treasure hunter. He was there when we were kids and I tried everything to get into the room. We all believed some fabulous pirate treasure waited inside. He could be the one who has Dotty."

9.

Detective Erik Lundgren promised to call Tyler back after he heard the story of Thomas' letter and Tyler's theory that Colin Currie kidnapped Dotty to get treasure from the Secret Room. Tyler explained there was no treasure. Erik said he'd call back. While we waited for Erik's follow-up call, I finally got the chance to ask Tyler about Colin.

Hunched forward with tension while he talked to Erik, Tyler loosened his shoulders and relaxed in the armchair, taking a deep breath before he answered. "Colin was our go-to guy for booze. He was the nerdy one, the smart one. Always had a way to make things happen. He told us he was filching liquor from his parents, that they were big party-givers who bought liquor by the case. They wouldn't notice if a bottle or two went missing."

"You didn't think stealing from parents was wrong?"

Tyler shrugged. "We wanted the booze, so we didn't ask questions. In fact, Colin was stealing from houses he thought were empty. Got caught, and when the cops came to his home, they found a huge stash of stolen liquor in his garage attic. He went to juvie for three months.

"Only then did we think Colin had done anything wrong. We stopped associating with him. Before that, hell, we all had reasons to be pissed off with parents. Didn't you? Yours went to Europe and left you on Spear Point."

I nodded. "I felt a little angry, especially when I got a postcard from my brother, Mark, at camp. He was deliriously happy collecting rocks in the mountains. I was so envious he was enjoying the summer."

"Your brother used to look for rocks here, I think," Tyler said. "I vaguely recall a summer when the little guy kept shoving stones at me, all excited by his finds. How's he doing?"

"The 'little guy' is 6'4". Mark's teaching geology at UCLA."

Tyler hmphed and set his phone on speaker. Our conversation lapsed, each of us with much to think about until Erik's call came in.

"I contacted the harbor master," Erik said. "He told me Colin's ship, the *Sand Dollar*, left Hopewell Harbor on the high tide this morning. They went to Damariscove Island. Will return with the tide on Sunday morning.

"Mrs. Hartley can't be on that ship. It's a 20-meter research vessel with six charter crew and seven expedition members. Cramped quarters; holds filled with gear. Not the place you'd stash a captive unless thirteen people were willing to risk their careers and freedom for one man's teenaged fantasy."

"But Damariscove's a treasure hunter's destination," Tyler said, "a pirate island. Colin's looking for treasure, not Viking artifacts."

"All kinds of ships landed and traded there. English, French, Dutch—even the Pilgrims—visited the island. Good chance Vikings found Damariscove, too."

"How do you know all this?" Tyler asked.

"I grew up here, Ty, not Boston, like you. We learned this stuff in school. And as for treasure…." Erik snorted. "Every island has its treasure tale—all bogus. Only Haskell Island panned out when a fishermen named Watson fell into a hole and landed on a kettle of gold."

"We're getting off point," I said. "What about Colin Currie?"

"Oh, hello, Megan. Didn't know you were there. I had the harbor master contact *Sand Dollar*'s captain. He said Colin stayed on shore.

"I think you're wrong about him, Ty," Erik added. "His record's clean after the teenaged conviction. He went on to Dartmouth, graduating with a degree in archaeology. He's been on a number of digs. His credentials are listed on The Viking Rediscovery Expedition website."

Tyler argued, "Rik, only guys in our group knew about the room in Dotty's house. One of them broke in."

The detective was silent for a moment before he said, "I noticed the house had changed from what I remember. Less furniture. Mrs. Hartley must have hired movers to haul away heavy pieces. They could have heard about the Secret Room. This is a small town; people talk. Our old friends have families, other friends. Everyone knew Mrs. Hartley had gone missing, and her house was supposed to be empty. Bottom line: You have not one shred of evidence connecting Colin Currie with Mrs. Hartley."

"What about the boot prints?" Tyler asked. "Colin's a small guy. Bet he's got those boots. Can't you seize them and check the dust against our cellar?"

Erik sighed. "I'll tell you why I don't want to do that. *If* Colin has the boots, we're talking criminal trespass, a misdemeanor—a nuisance charge."

"Damn it! I don't care about legal niceties. Dotty could be in danger right now. Maybe they intend to murder her and dump her body at sea."

"*They*," Erik said. "Who else do you think is involved?"

"I don't know! Someone Colin trusts."

"Okay, I don't believe Colin's mixed up in this, but you do, so let's run the scenario. First, Colin and Unnamed Henchman snatch Mrs. Hartley because they think she has treasure in the Secret Room. They need to know how to get in. She tells them a lie to play for time. Colin attempts to open the room but fails. He gets stuck in the cellar. Meanwhile, Henchman has gone to the library in town. Why?"

"He's looking for Thomas' instruction letter," Tyler said. "But it isn't in either place. The librarian has it in her purse."

Erik asked, "How do they know about the letter?"

"Maybe Colin saw Dotty using it when we were kids."

"Possibility. But, without the letter, what do they do next? Beat up Mrs. Hartley to get the truth?"

"Oh, God," I moaned.

"Too risky," Tyler said. "She's old. If they kill her, they don't have their answer."

"Right," said Erik. "Let's say they threaten her, and she gives them access. They must test the new information, but they now know people—you two—are in the way. You could identify them or even hold them at gunpoint."

"I don't have a gun," Tyler said.

"They don't know that. If they were sure Spear Point was deserted, they might try again, and we—I mean law enforcement—could nail them."

"But what about Dotty?" I asked. "What if they never tell us where she is?"

"You've just named one major problem. Here's another: When they find out there's no treasure, Mrs. Hartley is useless to them."

"I feel sick," I said.

"I feel better," Tyler said. "Everything points to Dotty being alive for now."

"Yes," said Erik. "Yes, it does, so we need to be careful about what we do next. Alerting Colin he's under suspicion by checking his boots could panic him into abandoning the whole scheme. That's when Mrs. Hartley's in real danger.

"Here's what I can do: Tomorrow, I'll call Colin at his parents' house. Welcome him back to Hopewell, invite him for a drink. His ship won't return until Sunday morning, according to the harbor master. We hoist some brews on Saturday night, and I sound him out on treasure hunting. I'll know if he's hedging or lying. Colin and I used to be tight; in fact, I was the one who got him started on Viking history. Lundgren, you know. Vikings are my peeps."

Erik's voice grew stern. "Neither of you is to talk with anyone—no one, including your parents, Megan—about this case. What you should do is work out how to get into the Secret Room. If nothing else, it'd be a good place to trap an intruder who might have Mrs. Hartley."

When Erik clicked off, I felt emotionally drained. "It's so complicated. So many *ifs*."

"At least, we have a plan, even if Rik's unconvinced we're moving in the right direction. In the morning, we go to Hopewell. I go to the post office for paperwork to stop Chloe's stalking, and then we visit Sam's Atlantic Antiques. I want to look at those bookcases again. When we get back, we figure out how to open the Secret Room." Tyler yawned, looked at his phone. "It's late. I'm going to bed. It'll be hard to sleep, but we have to try. Goodnight, Megs."

"Megs? We're friends now?"

He smiled, dimples and all. "Definitely."

I re-organized my bed. My tee shirt and lounge pants would do for pajamas. Tucked under Tyler's quilt, I breathed in his scent. It was nice, not an odor, just distinctly his chemistry. My dreams were all wrong for a person living the celibate life.

Tyler woke me by jostling my shoulder. "Megan, get up. It's five. We leave for Hopewell in one hour. It always takes women forever to get ready to go anywhere."

"Not me," I said. Determined to prove him wrong, I grabbed my toiletry bag and dashed to Dotty's house. I accomplished everything, including changing into a rumpled, navy Henley and white slacks, in twenty-four minutes. I'd have made my goal of thirty minutes if I hadn't forgotten my purse and had to go back for it.

"Amazing," Tyler said when I reached the cottage. He was locking up. "That was quick."

"I'm not vain."

"You should be."

I squinted at him. "Is that a compliment?"

He shrugged. "A bass ackwards one, I guess. Let's go."

The sun hadn't cleared the horizon yet, but the sky brightened as we drove. By the time we reached Hopewell, the lights were on at the General Store. Tyler suggested we grab coffee there. "Post Office won't open for another half hour."

I wasn't surprised to see Town Clerk Louise and Librarian Carla at their table in back. Tyler waved with the hand not holding a cinnamon roll. Kaitlyn brought coffee. Everything seemed so normal, I relaxed and contemplated the groceries I'd buy. Then, a thought struck me. "Ty, I should go to the library to look for the art book with the symbols. I didn't see it in Thomas' study. Dotty probably donated it."

"Talk to Carla. After I pay the tab, I'm on my way to the P.O."

I offered money, which Tyler waved away. When he left, I went to the ladies' table, introduced myself, fielded their questions about news on Dotty, and voiced condolences on the vandalism of the library. The librarian looked pleased about my interest, so I asked if I could look for a book in Dotty's donation boxes. "It's a sentimental favorite of mine," I said. "I'll pay whatever you expect from the sale."

"Nonsense," Carla said. "Dotty's been generous to the library. I won't take your money. It's a little early, but I'll open up now, and we'll see about your book."

We said goodbye to Louise, and then walked the block and a half to the library, a white, frame, two-story structure converted from a private home. Carla unlocked the door, which had a brass bell that tinkled as we entered, and she led me to the workroom in back.

"You'll have to dig through the boxes to find the one you want." She looked at me a moment, then tapped her lips. "I'm sure there was something I thought Tyler should have among the donations…but what was it?" She tilted her head and cupped her chin in her hand. "Oh, yes. That's right. It's the *Miller Family History*. Tyler's a Miller. He should keep it."

"Miller?" I said, thoroughly confused.

"His ancestors, I mean. Hiram Miller built the house on Spear Point."

"Oh! The one who married Amanda."

"If you say so. I'm no expert on the family, but it should all be in the book."

I gushed my thanks. Carla smiled sweetly, and left me to it. I pushed up my sleeves to start investigating the boxes. In the second one, I lucked out and found the *Miller Family History*. I yearned to look up Hiram and Amanda, but still needed the other book. Box six held *Signs and Symbols in Christian Art* by George Ferguson. Yes! I hugged it to my chest.

The front doorbell chimed. I heard footsteps, then a man's voice. "Miss Carla, you haven't changed a bit."

"Of course, I have, Colin, but it's nice of you to say so. It's been such a long time! Where have you been keeping yourself?"

"All over the world. I lead archaeological expeditions now."

Colin Currie! I stood by the door frame, peeking around it to get a look at him. Brown hair, not much taller than I, suntanned, wearing a white shirt, canvas pants, and work boots. One gold earring and wire-rimmed glasses. Afraid I'd be spotted, I ducked back into the room and shamelessly eavesdropped.

I heard Carla say, "You were always one of my favorites, Colin. Such an avid reader, unlike children today. I'm so glad things turned out well after that bit of unpleasantness. What can I do for you?"

"I need anything you have on Haskell Island, Miss Carla. I told my crew the story of the pot of gold, and they're dying to hear more. Internet info is sketchy."

"Easily done. I have a whole file on the subject. I'd rather it not leave the library, but we can make photocopies."

Hiding in the workroom, I pondered what to do. Colin Currie didn't know me; I could walk out the front door. But what if Carla mentioned Tyler? I'd rather not be linked to him. Better to stay anonymous.

I studied the back door. There was no wiring for an alarm. I slipped out with my books, vowing to make amends for my poor manners next time I saw the librarian.

After that, I ran to the antique shop. It was nearby, on the main street by the harbor. I wasn't even winded when I got there. I found Tyler just inside the doorway of Atlantic Antiques saying thanks to a middle-aged woman.

"Megan!" Tyler called, his voice jubilant. "Sam was polishing shelves of the bookcases. She discovered an inscription: SoS 4:12."

"SOS," I said. "Sounds like be a cry for help. Could Dotty have left a message?"

"No. There was grime in the grooves of the letters. They'd been there a long time. In fact…"

I stopped listening to Tyler as he stepped out to the sidewalk. Approaching us with a purposeful stride was an attractive blonde in a short, white dress. "Tyler!" she cried. "At last, I've found you." She closed the distance, and then, snaking her arms around his neck, simpered into his face. "We really need to get on with our courtship. I have so many plans."

Tyler's reaction was instant. "Get off me!" He tore her arms away from his throat.

Big, round, brown eyes looked up at him undaunted. "Well, that's no way to greet your fiancée. It's very rude."

"You are *not* my fiancée." Tyler's voice turned hard. "All I want from you is an answer: Where's my grandmother, Chloe?"

She shrugged. "How should I know? Careless of you to lose her."

Tyler's face went red; his body tensed. I was afraid he would hit her, but all he did was shove her away.

"Tsk, Tsk." Chloe clucked her tongue. "I don't like how you're behaving. I could have you arrested for assault."

There was my cue. I stepped forward. "Excellent idea, Miss Goode, getting law enforcement involved, I mean. Never mind that Mr. Hartley has two defense witnesses."

I tapped my chest and then pointed to Sam, who stood frankly gawking in her doorway. To Sam, I said, "Take pictures, will you?" She pulled out her phone and aimed it at the three of us, clicking off half a dozen shots before she withdrew into the shop.

Chloe turned to me, dropping her winsome, sweet act. "Who're you?"

"Mr. Hartley's lawyer. We're on our way to West Bath, where he will file a petition for a Protection from Harassment Order against you with the District Court under Title 5 *Maine Revised Statutes*, Section 4651. Later, it's onward to Brunswick, where he'll lodge a criminal complaint for stalking under Title 17-A *M.R.S.* §210-A. Both will require inquiry. After they scrutinize your life—ferreting out *all* your secrets—conviction mandates at least a year in jail.

"But really," I said, speaking confidentially to her, "don't you deserve a better man? One who's thrilled to have you? Mr. Hartley…well, he's not the faithful type."

Chloe stood there with her mouth open. Finally, she answered in the tone of a child denied candy, "But we're soulmates."

"You were matched by a computer with incomplete data. Now," I said, "ready to make your complaint?"

She frowned at Tyler. She gave me a withering look. "You think you're so smart, but I'm smart, too. You haven't seen the last of me." With that, she turned on her heel and strode off. I lost sight of her when she rounded the corner across from the General Store.

Staring at me, Tyler said, "You're incredible! How did you know such stuff? You had me convinced you're a lawyer."

"I did the research yesterday, and I am a lawyer. Not licensed in Maine, of course, but in Illinois. Didn't I tell you I lived in Chicago when I was married?"

"No. And I didn't ask." Tyler took my arm as we walked toward the General Store. "I feel stupid. We've been together nearly three days, and I never once asked what you do."

"It's all right. We've had a lot on our minds."

"That's no excuse," Tyler objected. "I'm that guy at a party who only talks about himself—total bore. I mean—" He stopped his self-rebuke when we reached his car in front of the General Store. A white paper was stuck under the passenger-side wiper blade. "Oh, crap. A ticket."

He plucked the paper free. Tyler read, then handed me, a printed note: Leave the stone behind the buoy shack by midnight and clear out. Make sure you're not followed.

"Stone?" we asked each other.

10.

A bejeweled hand thrust between Tyler and me. Louise snatched the paper from my grasp saying, "Oh, honestly! A ticket at this hour? When you're parked legally? Outrageous. I'll take care of it."

Tyler spoke to her like a father who'd found his toddler toying with a carving knife. "That's not for you, Louise."

She ignored him while she read the paper. Looking up, she whispered, "This isn't a ticket. It's…it's a ransom note."

"We think so," Tyler said.

"But there's no mention of Dotty," I said. "It's just a demand for a stone."

Louise passed the note to Tyler. "Well, at least they don't want anything important. Why anyone would want that rock is beyond me."

"Stone or rock could mean a large gem," I said.

Louise waved her hand dismissively. Her bracelets jangled. "Dotty doesn't like gemstones. Thinks they're vulgar, prefers pearls. No, she only has one stone—an ordinary rock from Spear Point her nephew found years ago. It made her smile to remember how proud he was when he gave it to her."

"I should call my brother," I said. "Maybe Mark remembers his gift. What time is it in California?"

Tyler checked his phone. "4:45 a.m."

"Oh. I'll have to call later. What does this rock look like, Louise?"

"It's ordinary, though it has some graffiti on. Maybe the little boy tried scratching in his name. Dotty kept it in the parlor on the cabinet under the ghastly mirror that made everyone look short and fat."

"Oh, I know the one!" Tyler said. Then he frowned. "The cabinet went to Sam's antique shop, but I have no idea what happened to the rock."

"Check the garden," Louise advised. "I suggested Dotty put it there when she mentioned she was moving things out of the room. I mean, weather can't harm a rock."

Tyler looked at me. "It's worth a shot." He favored Louise with his best smile and thanked her. She stood on the curb beaming at him until he said, "Uh, Louise, could you step back so Megan can get in the car?"

We left her staring after us as we drove out of town.

Once we'd left Hopewell and were on the open road, I asked Tyler, "Do you think it's too much of a coincidence that Louise was there to direct us to the stone? Could she be a part of this?"

"No." Tyler shook his head vehemently. "Never. Louise is one of Dotty's best friends. She came out of the General Store, thought she should cancel an unfair ticket, and made an educated guess."

"But what if she's wrong? What if we piss off the note writer by leaving a worthless stone by the buoy shack?"

"Hmm. Well, we'll leave our own note saying we've tried to follow directions. If they want something else, we need a better description.

"And beggars can't be choosers," Tyler went on. "All they did was tell us to leave a stone. They're not promising to give Dotty back. I don't even know why we're doing this."

"Because if we don't, and Dotty's harmed, we'll be responsible. I still think there must be something valuable involved—a piece of jewelry, probably, one Dotty didn't tell Louise about. With Dotty's jewelry in the Secret Room, we *have* to get inside to know for sure."

"No time. With any luck, we'll find the graffiti stone with just enough leeway to turn back to town before the tide cuts us off. I say we put it by the shack immediately, not wait for midnight."

"Good idea, but I'm staying at Spear Point," I said. "You take the stone to Hopewell. Then you should go to the District Court and the Sheriff's Office to make your Chloe complaints. If you delay, she'll think we were bluffing."

"You're not coming with me?" Tyler risked a glance away from the road to check my reaction.

"Can't. You'll be all right on your own, though. You have the papers from your lawyer. All you need do now is copy them and fill in what happened today, unless—Other than today, did Chloe bother you after your break up with Nicole?"

"No. Maybe she lost track of me. I sublet my apartment and rented a room in a private house. Just wanted a place to sleep, wash up and dress. Threw myself into work while I licked my wounds."

"Be sure to put that in your complaint. Being forced out of your residence by a stalker is serious, will get attention. And just think: Once you shake Chloe off your tail, maybe you can patch things up with Nicole."

"That ship has sailed," Tyler said. "Last time I saw Nicole, she was in the apartment building lobby wrapped around some guy who was holding Molly's hand."

"Oh. She moved on."

"Yep. And after my firm changed to a four-day week, I moved up here last fall when Dotty sold the Lizzie. I didn't want her stuck without transportation all winter."

"Dotty sold the Lizzie? No! I loved that car."

"So did Dotty, but she decided an ancient Model T needed more care than she could provide. Sold Lizzie to a collector in Boston, I think."

"Too bad." I shook off my grief and focused on the task at hand. "Once we find the stone, you need to call Erik Lundgren to tell him about the note."

"Are you sure? Police involvement might drive the note writer away. I thought I'd settle in somewhere among the trees and keep watch—see who turns up."

"Uh-uh. Nope. You're unarmed, and you're not a cop. Erik's the one for this job."

"You don't think I can handle it?" Tyler asked, his voice sharp.

Oh, dear. Affronted masculinity. Time to change the subject. "Uh, I forgot to tell you I saw Colin Currie at the library. He wanted information about the Haskell Island treasure."

"I knew it!" Tyler crowed. "Knew he was after pirate treasure, not Viking artifacts."

"Maybe he's the letter writer," I said, hatching a new idea as I spoke. "Louise said the stone has graffiti on it. Could it be a marker or a treasure map?"

"There've been no rumors of treasure at Spear Point. Why would a map or marker or whatever be there?"

"I don't know, but it's the best explanation I can come up with for someone wanting a common stone." I looked at the books I'd taken from the library, now sitting in my footwell. "Maybe there was talk of treasure in the past. Might be info in this book on your family."

Naturally, Tyler wanted to know what book and why I had it. I answered his questions about the *Miller Family History* as best I could, ending with, "I hope we'll find something on ghostly Amanda, too."

Talked out, and processing too many thoughts, I stayed silent for the rest of the drive. On the causeway to Spear Point, I saw the water was rising. We'd have to hurry to find the stone.

Reaching the house, we parked, and went to the garden. I was all for walking the rows of vegetables, then the flowers, to search for the stone, but Tyler had another idea. "Follow me," he said, striding toward the far end of the flower beds. "Something important to Dotty would be here." He pointed to a mound of stones. "This is where she buried Huntley."

"Oh, Huntley…I remember him. Sweet dog." He'd been a puppy when I spent the summer at Dotty's seventeen years ago. A somewhat timid dog, Huntley was devoted to Dotty, hardly ever leaving her side.

"He lived to be ten. Great dog to the end." Tyler bent to study the stone pile.

"She built him a cairn," I mused. "What a nice memorial."

"And here," Tyler said, "just as I expected, is a rock with lines on it." He looked at the rock, then handed it to me.

It was gray, about nine inches long, and flat on one side. The lines resembled letters, maybe a word: MIRIYR. "If Mark carved the rock, he must have been really young. Doesn't look a lot like his name."

Tyler shrugged. "Maybe he'll have an explanation when you call him. It's going on six in California now."

"Still early," I said, "and it'll be a long call because I'll have to fill him in on what's happened here. You checked for other stones? Yes? Then, I guess we have what we need." I took photos of the stone, then reminded Tyler, "You'd better get moving to outrun the incoming tide."

"You're right." He turned toward the car, then stopped to wait for me. By the front of the house, he said, "I don't like leaving you here alone. Any other time, sure. Nothing to worry about, but too much stuff has happened. If you feel anything's off—even just a little—go to the shed and lock yourself in." He reached into his pocket, pulled out his keyring, and worked one key free. "If you do go in, take the lock with you. There's a steel door bar inside. Lower it, and no one's getting in. You'll have cell tone, though. I made connection a design priority."

He looked at me. I looked at him. He said, "Don't lose the key," and then he reached out with one hand. I didn't know if he meant to shake my hand or pat my arm or what. I took the initiative and hugged him. When we separated, he looked surprised but pleased. He smiled, got into the car, and drove off.

I realized that, despite my teenaged fantasies, I'd never felt Tyler's arms around me before. It was a first time, but I hoped it wouldn't be the last. I grinned as I picked up my purse and books from the front steps.

When I entered Thomas' study, I felt leery about sitting at the desk. Dotty didn't have many house rules, but touching Thomas' desk was strictly off limits to everyone. She didn't say it, and yet we knew, the desk was a shrine to her dead husband. She kept a pad of lined paper and a sharpened pencil on top, as though he might dash in to jot down notes at any minute.

In the past, the room held other chairs, but those were gone now. I had no choice but to use the desk chair or sit on the floor. Still, I worked off my anxiety by picking up books the vandal scattered. Only when they were shelved did I venture toward the desk.

Thomas' wooden chair was surprisingly comfortable, with its recessed seat, bowed back slats and gently curved top rail. The desk's knee well was wide enough to accommodate the chair's armrests, so

I could roll in close to the desktop.

Before I did that, I noted the desk's unusual design. Instead of one wide, shallow drawer in the middle, there were three filling the top level. Wondering why Thomas wanted separate compartments, I peeked inside them. All empty. No clues there. So, I used the pencil to draw on the pad, making a plan of the room as it had been before most of the bookcases were removed.

I drew three lines for the walls I could see: right/west, front/south and left/east. I ignored the north wall behind me because it never had bookcases, just a credenza beneath high windows. Next, I drew two bookcases on the right, three in front, and two to the left.

Eying the rose symbol on the cases to my left, I saw it was divided, with half a flower on one case and half on the other. I remembered the carvings on all the cases had been bisected.

As I drew in symbols for the cases from right to left, I noticed they matched Thomas' letter—heart, anchor, cross, rose. I had the order, but what was I to do with it?

I leaned on my hands, studied the drawing, then pushed back in the chair. After a frustrated sigh, I sat forward and cried, "C'mon Thomas! Throw me a bone here. *Please.* I'm trying to help Dotty, but I need help."

Of course, I got no answer. The only change in the room was a dimming of light from the windows. Looking over my shoulder, I saw the gloomy, overcast sky finally decided to send down rain. I heard a patter of drops on the panes.

Wishing I had a lamp, I pulled the pad upright to see it better. That's when everything made sense. The placement of bookcases in the room and the arrangement of desk drawers were identical. This was no coincidence. Dotty could discard the bookcases because they didn't control access to the Secret Room: The desk did.

I yelled, "Yes!" and then said a quiet, "Thanks," to Thomas. Maybe he heard me. Who knows? At any rate, I now had to figure out how to use those drawers.

My first choice was to pull them out, one at a time, from bottom right across the top to bottom left. Nothing happened. I shut all the drawers after making sure they were empty.

Once again, I contemplated Thomas' letter. He'd gone on and on about how much inspiration Dotty was for him. She was his other half. Together, they were a pair, like the divided symbols.

Two. Two was important. I'd try two drawers at a time. Right side, check. Top right and middle, check. But what about the drawer on the end? I shrugged, pulled it out, then went for the last set.

Still nothing. I was missing something, and I had a feeling it was the third drawer, all by its lonesome. How could I make a pair out of one?

I tried again, opening one pair, then two. Next, instead of opening the third drawer by itself, I closed the middle one and pulled both middle and left together. When I moved the left drawers, I heard a click and the sound of a motor behind the rose bookcases—inside the Secret Room.

By the time I dashed to the east wall, a gap appeared as the cases moved apart, one going left and one right. When the gap spread about three inches, I saw metal tracks on the floor, clearly the mechanism moving the bookcases. Tapping my foot, I watched another inch of opening appear and then the cases stopped. The motor noise changed to an irritated whine, and I smelled ozone, signaling an overload.

What to do? What to do? Something must be blocking the track. No way would I stick my fingers under the cases to find out. I rushed back to the desk to get the pencil, which I slid under the left case. It moved freely, but when I tried the same test on the right side, the pencil stuck about four feet from center.

I swore, sat back on my heels, and knew I had to turn the motor off before it burned out. Peering into the gap, I could see nothing in the darkness, so I went back to the desk and closed the drawers in reverse order. The bookcases returned to their original positions. I heard a click, and then, blessed silence.

Needing to share the bad news, I called Tyler to explain what I'd learned and done, ending with the stuck bookcase problem.

"Probably the uneven floor," Tyler opined. "Wait till I get there, and—"

"How about a tool?" I cut in.

"You could try a crowbar. I have one in the shed."

"Crowbar for such a heavy case?"

"Leverage. That's what they're good for. Likely a longshot, though. If the obstruction's not too high and outside the track, you could use a chisel and mallet to shave it down."

"But I would damage the floor."

"So, hold off and let me have a look. Low tide's around five."

I knew I wouldn't wait. I wanted into that room—*now*. Ending the conversation as soon as I could, I locked up the house, sprinted to the shed, opened the substantial padlock and carried it with me inside, where I barred the door as Tyler instructed. I swiped raindrops from my face and shook my head at my own paranoia.

Ceiling lights came on. *Slick. Must be a sensor*, I thought. The room was comfortable, not muggy or hot. Climate control, as Tyler had said.

The paved, cinder block interior was divided into two sections with an aisle between. To my right was Tyler's office furniture and equipment, followed by a pile of jumbled boxes with sporting goods and men's clothing hanging out. Obviously, Tyler's stuff. Beyond this was a workbench with pegboard and neatly arranged tools. In the back corner, an open area before a wide door contained Dotty's electric bike, leaving ample room for Tyler's car.

On the other side were boxes, all fresh and sealed, plus some furniture way at the back. Dotty's collections? Must be. I'd learned a bit about boxes when I moved from Illinois to Florida. I spotted a row of dish drums in front, then row after row of book boxes and two-foot squares. Beyond these were larger, narrow mirror boxes. At the very back, on a table, lay long, white rectangles I hadn't seen in the box store.

My mother had asked me to check on Dotty's collections to see if they were valuable enough to support her in her old age. I should do that now, I decided, even if it meant delaying my attempt to open the Secret Room.

There were no labels on the boxes, only numbers. My snooping would have ended there if I hadn't seen a clipboard hanging from a hook on the wall. Sure enough, it held a paper inventory.

Okay, so first boxes were Royal Doulton, Wedgwood, Limoges. Dotty had some nice china. *A lot* of nice china. Next came: Waterford, Lalique, Tiffany. Crystal or glass. Christofle, Revere, Sheffield, Gorham. Had to be silver. Art 17c, 18c, 19c, 20c were followed by First editions, Documents and Stamps. There were names I didn't recognize until I came to Isfahan, Kirman, Mughal, which could only be carpet rolls on the floor where I couldn't see them. The last entry was Gowns.

At this point, I felt like I'd wandered into a museum storage room. The sensation got worse when I approached the gowns. The white boxes were meant for archival preservation, the kind women sometimes use for wedding dresses. But these were marked Poiret, Vionnet, Lanvin, Worth.

Charles Frederick Worth—the most famous designer of the Nineteenth Century? He invented couture fashion, and dressed royalty. Through the cellophane window, I saw what looked like a ball gown of rose silk, black velvet and ivory lace. Exquisite.

With some effort (because my knees were shaking), I made my way back to Tyler's desk chair and called him. I only gave him time to answer before I said, "Tyler, just one question: Are you aware Dotty's collections are worth a fortune?"

11.

I expected Tyler to be shocked, or to tell me he knew. Instead, I heard crowd noises around him .“Uh, yeah, okay. I’m kind of into something here. It’s—”

He was interrupted by a male voice saying, “I got you wheat beer. Okay, Ty?”

I *knew* that voice. I heard it just this morning. Tyler was with Colin Currie.

“Sure, fine.” To me, Tyler said, “I’ll call you back.” Click.

Sitting there in the shed, I scowled and drummed my fingers on the desk. Tyler and Colin were meeting in a bar somewhere. Tyler said they hadn’t been friends since their teenaged years. He’d accused Colin of breaking into the house, writing the note, and even kidnapping Dotty. Colin was a sketchy character, so why were the two of them hoisting brews together? Were they planning something?

It was Tyler who told Dotty to move heavy things out of her house; Tyler who rebuilt the carriage shed. Now Dotty’s valuables were neatly boxed, all in one place. How easy it would be to load them into a truck and haul them away—especially with Dotty absent.

I jumped up from the chair to grab the inventory sheets and put them under box 7 for this month, July, the seventh month of the year. I’d remember the number, but thieves wouldn’t know what was in the boxes.

My phone buzzed. I thought it was Tyler. “What?” I snapped.

"Megan?" Not Tyler's voice. "It's Erik Lundgren. Everything all right there?"

Should I tell him about my suspicions? I had no evidence, so I said, "Sorry. Thought you were someone else."

"Glad I'm not. Sounds like someone's in trouble," Erik said lightly. "I'm calling to tell you Ty gave me the stone. I'll put it by the shack at dusk, and then do a stakeout to see who comes for it."

"Good. I really want to know who's behind that note."

"Have you talked to your brother? Ty said he's the one who found the stone."

"Not yet."

"When you do, be sure to ask where he got it."

"Why is that important?"

"I'm not sure," Erik admitted, "but details can matter to a case. Oh, and one more thing: Are we still on for a boat ride and dinner tomorrow?"

I was in no mood for a date with Erik, which I had made mostly to spite Tyler. "Um, a night out doesn't seem right when Dotty's still missing. Feels disrespectful. And, I'm only here for a short time. I'll be off to Florida when we find her, so I don't want to get anything started."

"Okay, so no date. How about we just share a meal? I enjoy good food, but it's awkward to eat by myself, and take-outs aren't the same, you know?"

I did know. After the divorce, I missed fine dining. I could never get my female friends to agree to a fancy meal. They didn't want to dress up or didn't want to spend the money, generally arguing we should go "someplace casual".

"I hear you," I told Erik. "But—"

"Just think about it. After you contact your brother, please give me a call. Bye for now."

I pocketed my phone and found tools that might get me into the Secret Room. Outside, hard rain was falling. Before I made it to the house, I was soaked.

Leaving crowbar, chisel and mallet by the front door, I went to change into dry clothes and towel my hair. I felt cold, lonely and conflicted. I needed to hear a friendly voice.

In the kitchen, I noticed I was famished, hadn't eaten since early morning. Meditatively munching a pb&j sandwich, I called my brother, hoping he wasn't in the middle of teaching a geology class.

"Meg?" Mark asked, his voice alarmed. "You all right? Mom and Dad okay?"

I made a mental note to call my brother more often so he wouldn't always expect a crisis. Sadly, this call couldn't be reassuring. I told Mark about Dotty and the mysterious note.

"Wow. I'll book a flight to Maine."

"Hold off on that. We have enough boots on the ground. You can help by telling me about this." I sent him pictures of the stone.

Once he got them, Mark said, "I remember that find. I must have been six or seven, poking around the grotto, where I shouldn't have been—Mom was afraid I'd drown in the pool. Insisted I stay away unless someone was with me, but that day, I just had to go rock hunting.

"One stone caught my eye. First thing I saw was an M, my initial. I was intrigued, but I couldn't read the rest of the word."

"You're sure it's a word?" I asked.

"I'm sure the letters are manmade. Those aren't natural fissures. Schist is a metamorphic rock compressed by high temperature and pressure. It fractures along its layers, not against the grain."

"So, when you found the stone…" I prompted.

"I took it to Aunt Dotty, hoping she could tell me what the marks meant. She said it wasn't an English word but the rock still looked special, so I gave it to her. She hugged me and fed me cookies." Mark sighed. "Why would anyone want to harm her? Aunt Dotty's such a good person."

"We'll find her," I said.

Mark went silent a while before he said, "You know, Aunt Dotty told me the word wasn't English. What about another language? All those consonants look kind of Slavic. I'll go over to the Eastern European Languages Department to see if anyone there can make sense of the letters."

"Great idea. And Mark, Mom and Dad don't know about the note. They can't help, but Mom's blood pressure would go through the roof."

"Gotcha. Just keep me in the loop. Be careful, Megs. I don't want anything happening to you."

It's amazing how a little support from someone you love and trust can renew the spirit, rebuild emotional strength. I promised myself when Tyler showed up, my doubts wouldn't be sidelined by glib answers. I'd demand the truth about whatever he was doing with Colin.

For now, I had work to do. I went to the hall to reclaim the tools, then stopped. *Should* I try to unblock the door and open the Secret Room? Last night, the detective warned us a kidnapper expecting treasure in the room but finding none might decide he no longer needed Dotty's information—or Dotty. Better to leave the room closed.

Stupidly, I told Tyler I cracked the code, but hadn't explained the process step by step. I skipped over the details. Good. Still, he knew I knew, and maybe that put me at risk. I didn't like that thought at all.

Getting into the room had been just a puzzle to solve for me. Tyler could have another motive. He told me the room held no treasure, but what if it did? How slick it would be to steal a treasure no one believed was real, no one would miss?

Except Dotty. And Dotty wasn't here.

I hustled to Thomas' study, tore off the page of my drawing and several other sheets so there'd be no impressions on the pad. In the kitchen, I swished the pages in soapy water until the graphite was gone. After ripping the papers into small pieces, I shoved them under food waste in the garbage bin. No one but me would know how to access the Secret Room.

Returning to the study to think, I realized Thomas' desk no longer intimidated me. If anything, I felt he and I were on the same team. He'd want me to keep doing all I could for Dotty.

I wondered how the rumors of treasure got started. Were there pirates in the family? I consulted the *Miller Family History*.

The book was deadly dull, starting with the Norman Conquest of England. Like every family of English descent in America, the Millers claimed William the Conqueror as their ancestor. Skipping through the years, I slowed when I got to the Eighteenth Century, the Golden Age of Piracy. Unsurprisingly, no Millers were listed as pirates or privateers. This book was written by a Miller for Millers. It was a puff piece, intended to elevate the family, not to air dirty laundry.

More dreary pages followed until I reached the Nineteenth Century and spotted Hiram Miller, the man who'd built this house.

Hiram Miller (1817-1888), fisherman, was born to Alva and Olive Miller of Haskell Island. He acquired wealth in his later years. In 1860, he married Amanda Watson (1837-1864), only child of John and Mary Watson, also of Haskell Island. She bore him

> three children: Harwood, Clara, and Richard. Harwood (1861-1915) became a notable businessman. Clara (1863-1933) married State Senator Tybalt Rutledge. Richard (1864-1885) died at State Hospital after a long illness.

That brief description raised a lot of questions. How had Hiram "acquired wealth"? And the name—Amanda Watson, the Amanda who became our ghost. She had to be the daughter of the man who found pirate gold. Maybe she inherited some of her father's loot, and that's how the treasure story started. But so much time had passed. How could any pirate treasure still remain?

Thomas' note used the word *treasure*, too. He'd written, "You are the key to my happiness, my treasure." Since all his endearments had been meaningful, his reference to treasure wasn't accidental.

Damn. All I wanted was to find Dotty, not deal with treasure-hunters or thieves. I stretched my arms, shrugged my shoulders. I needed to work off some of the tension I felt.

I did what I always do when I'm upset: clean. Starting with the kitchen, I mopped and scrubbed, then moved to the dining room and study to ply feather duster and the motorless Fuller carpet sweeper. Next, I tackled the parlor. I was polishing furniture when I heard the front doorbell ring, though ring is an overstatement. The old, manual twist device chirped like a bicycle bell.

I went to the hall where I heard Tyler shout, "Megan, let me in. It's pouring out here."

"No," I yelled through the door. "You met with Colin Currie."

"Yeah, and a good thing, too. We cleared the air. Shit, Megan, I'm getting drenched."

"I don't care! The two of you are up to something."

"What are you talking about?"

"Means, motive and opportunity. You and Colin—co-conspirators."

Silence, then, "Colin told me what he's really doing, but if I can't come in, I'll go home."

I growled. Tyler knew how to push my buttons, knew curiosity would win over caution. I moved the crowbar I'd left in the hall away from the door. He came in, stamped water off his shoes, slicked back dripping hair and glowered at me.

"You have five minutes to convince me you're not plotting against Dotty," I said.

"Or what?" He eyed the crowbar. "You'll bash in my head?"

I rolled my eyes. "Five minutes."

"Point one." Tyler held up his index finger for emphasis. "I'm not conspiring with Colin. I met with him because Rik told me to. He planned to have drinks with Colin but couldn't go because of the stone. Had to figure out surveillance and arrange for backup and, I dunno, police stuff. Rik told me to keep the appointment.

"Two: Colin had nothing to do with Dotty's disappearance. He was on the ship in another part of Maine the day she vanished.

"Three: Colin didn't send the note. Looked blank when I mentioned it.

"Four: He did break into this house or, in his words, 'entered without permission'—"

"A lesser charge," I noted.

"…to get inside the Secret Room and look for pirate treasure. He thought there might be a button or switch on the bookcases, so he moved the books."

"Threw them around the room, you mean."

"These are *my* five minutes, Megan, so stop interrupting," Tyler said testily. "Okay, so, uh, Colin went upstairs to check if there were a way in from above, like a hatch. Pretty smart. I never thought of that. Anyway, he heard you, panicked because the house was supposed to be empty, hid in the cellar until everything was quiet, then left. He crossed the causeway on foot in the moonlight, going to the car he'd hidden nearby."

"He's delusional," I said. "Obsessed with pirates, like some little boy."

"I don't think so. He made a good case for treasure being here. It seems John Watson wasn't the only one to find pirate gold on Haskell Island. Hiram Miller found another kettle with coins."

"Another kettle? How does Colin know about this?"

"His ancestor worked as housekeeper for Watson. She gossiped with her daughter, who later told her granddaughter, who wrote down the story. Miller wanted to marry Amanda Watson, but her dad said no; Miller wasn't rich enough. Miller searched for more treasure and found it."

"Then he married Watson's only child," I added.

"Right. Now Colin's desperate to satisfy his expedition backers. To date, his crew has found nothing. Sponsors, he says, don't like spending their money and getting zilch results. A coin from Hiram's stash would make the case there were several treasure hoards on the island so there could be more."

"He's going to claim he found the gold? That's fraud. And why would he break in just to take one coin? Why not steal them all?"

"Colin didn't intend to steal the treasure. He just had to know if it was here. Sure, he wants to keep his expedition gig going, but burglary would land him in jail, so he told me what he did and asked for my help. If Dotty were here, he'd have asked her."

I frowned. "Wasn't he supposed to be looking for Viking artifacts?"

"Yes, but Colin says it's like searching for the Holy Grail. It'd change history if he could prove Norse explorers reached Maine, but no one's found irrefutable evidence. He knew it was a long, long, long shot, yet he gave it a try." Tyler paused for breath, then asked, "Do we have to keep standing here in the hall?"

"Go to the kitchen. I'll follow you."

Tyler preceded me through the parlor and dining room, only looking over his shoulder once. I got the distinct impression he thought I'd lost my mind.

He sat at the kitchen table; I stood. "Why are you so concerned about a man you haven't seen in years?" I asked.

"Because I owe him. Colin thought we—his friends—dropped him when he was caught stealing and wasn't useful to us anymore. I told him he had it wrong. We were afraid we'd get in trouble, too. We ghosted him because we were cowards. I apologized."

"Sweet of you," I said, "but he hasn't really changed his ways. He sneaked into this house like a thief. Why should we believe he wasn't here to rob Dotty when he thought he could get away with it?"

"If Dotty had coins, she'd give him one. She liked Colin, believed he'd gotten a raw deal. But all of this is moot. We don't have treasure," Tyler said. "Look, would you please sit down?"

I sat. "I have a feeling there's more than you've told me. I don't want to be tricked."

"You aren't going to be tricked by me."

I crossed my arms, scouring his eyes, trying to look into his mind. He met my scrutiny without wavering. "I'm not the enemy. We're on the same side."

"How can I know that? How can I be sure you're telling me the truth?"

Tyler laid his hand on mine. "I've never lied to you. Probably will, sometime in the future, about a bad haircut or a culinary disaster, but not about something important. Never about Dotty. She's the only family I have, the only one who really cares about me."

I moved my hand, looked away. "Not the only one," I mumbled.

"What?"

"Nothing."

Next thing I knew, Tyler's fingertips were turning my chin. He brushed my lips with his. Surprised and flustered, I jerked away, saying, "What was *that* for?"

"Because I heard what you said." He offered his best, most beautiful, most devastating smile, then announced, "I'm going home to dry off, warm up. Just have this one, big question…."

Wide-eyed, I leaned forward.

"Where do you think Dotty keeps umbrellas?"

12.

An hour later, I stood on the cottage doorstep gripping a casserole dish between hot pads. "Tyler," I called, "I'm here to apologize, and I've brought you dinner."

He opened the door. "What's this?"

"Dotty's recipe for spaghetti, homemade sauce and meatballs. There's garlic bread, too." I lowered my chin. "This afternoon I gave you a hard time, so I'll understand if you've had enough of me for one day. I won't stay."

"Don't be silly. Come in."

"You're sure?"

"I'm sure. I accept your apology, I'm hungry, and I want your company." He moved aside so I could enter.

"I need something to put under this. Don't want to burn your counter," I said.

Tyler pulled a dish towel from over the faucet and laid it on the kitchen table. I settled the dish, then slipped Dotty's fabric shopping bag from my arm to pull out foil-wrapped garlic bread. Tyler took two bottled ice teas from the frig.

"Smells good," he said. "I haven't eaten since breakfast if you don't count bar pretzels." He set the table, handing me serving spoon and fork for the spaghetti. I gave him a hefty portion.

Tyler scarfed down half his plate before asking, "This is Dotty's recipe? When did she teach you cooking?"

"When I was here for the summer. On a rainy day like today, I was bored to tears. She told me she needed my help. As if. I mostly watched, but it was fun. My mother never shares her kitchen. It's her exclusive domain."

"Your mother's missing out." Tyler took another bite, chewed, then asked, "Ready to tell me why you went dark today? Why you were so, uh…."

"Paranoid?" I frowned, considering the question. "It was the collections. The makers Dotty listed are the best of the best. All those boxes in one place would make a nice haul for a thief. You told her to put them there."

"I had no idea," Tyler said. "Just thought she had a lot of old lady stuff. You know, knickknacks, pictures, faded books and clothes, travel souvenirs. Maybe she wanted to save some of those Victorian nasties." He wrinkled his nose. "Like the hair wreath and stuffed raven and—"

"Don't remind me. But I think something else was goading me on. I'm afraid of seeing what I want to see, then learning it's not true. Like my life with Chase. For the longest time, I thought it would work out, kept believing he'd grow up, but the older he got, the more he wanted to be a boy. Afterward, I felt foolish, ashamed I hadn't caught on sooner."

"I'm not Chase," Tyler said. "I don't think my best days are behind me. Could be, they're just ahead."

He held me with his gaze, asking an unspoken question I couldn't answer, so I changed the subject. "What I can't understand is how Dotty could afford such fine things. Her parents weren't rich. She worked as a teacher. Her husband was in government service." A thought occurred to me. "Could Thomas have gotten into something illegal? Was he killed because he crossed the wrong people?"

"Oh, great. My grandfather the spy was also a crook. What other skeletons will we find in the closet?" He eyed the spaghetti dish. "Mind if I have more?"

"Go ahead. I made this for you."

He helped himself, and then asked, "Any coins in Dotty's boxes?"

"None that I saw."

"Too bad, because today, well, I did something I might need to explain."

"The kiss?"

He looked surprised. "No, that's simple. I kissed you because I wanted to. Did I overstep?"

I shook my head. He smiled, adorable dimples and all. "No, this is about my telling Colin he could see inside the Secret Room tomorrow. I asked him to come with me this afternoon, but he had a date tonight."

"Fast worker," I observed, "if he's only been in town one day."

"Must be a fix-up. Colin has four sisters."

"Ah. Still, maybe it's too soon," I argued. "We haven't opened the room, and Erik told us not to let anyone know it was empty."

"He said not to let a *kidnapper* know it was empty. Colin's no kidnapper. His ship wasn't anywhere near Hopewell when Dotty went missing."

"He could have an accomplice. Someone broke into the library the same night he was here, remember?"

"The library intruder might be after the stone and not connected to Colin at all." Tyler looked out the window. "Sun should set in another hour, hour and a half. With any luck, Rik will catch the note writer and we'll have our answer tonight."

"About Erik," I said, sipping the last of my tea, "I'm supposed to go to dinner with him tomorrow."

"I'd rather you didn't."

"Why?"

"I'm selfish. I like eating dinner with you."

I smiled. "Maybe I'll beg off, though I hate to lie. Oh, speaking of liars, how'd the Chloe paperwork go?"

"District court was a bust. Office I needed was closed until Monday. I did file my complaint with the Sheriff's Department. They said they'd come if she harassed me, but they couldn't look for her without a picture. I didn't have one."

"Yes, you do. Sam took pictures at the antique shop today."

"Of course!" He picked up his phone and sent a text to Sam.

I reached for Tyler's plate to carry it with mine to the sink, but he held onto it. "Can't leave one lone piece of garlic bread." After he chomped the bread, he said, "I just realized how bad my breath must be."

"Mine, too," I admitted ruefully.

"Mint ice cream?" Tyler grinned. "Just happen to have some."

We gorged on local, hand-made ice cream. I asked about doing dishes, but Tyler decided they could wait. "We should get working on the Secret Room."

"Now? After all that spaghetti?

"Be a waste to have Colin out to Spear Point if the doors won't open. He's scheduled to leave tomorrow night. I'm sure he'd rather spend time with family if there's nothing to see here."

Tyler gathered some items he wanted into the grocery sack, and we went into the living room. I saw the mess I'd left from my overnight visit.

As I stood by the couch, I felt Tyler's hands on my shoulders, then gliding down my arms until he took my hands in his. He said into my ear, "You don't have to go back to Dotty's. You could stay with me."

"Another glorious night on the couch," I quipped.

"Wherever you want."

And there it was: my open invitation. Did I want to sleep with Tyler? Hell, yes. Was I going to?

I turned, touched his cheek. "You are *such* a temptation," I mused aloud, "but I'm not good with casual hookups, friends with benefits, whatever. I get attached, and I can't be pining for a man fifteen hundred miles away."

"Pining?"

"Yeah," I confessed. "It'd be bad."

"Florida's only a couple hours by plane."

I shook my head. "Long distance never works out. You imagine nothing will change, but a couple months later, you hear, 'I met someone.'"

"You're overthinking."

"You know I'm right."

If he'd kissed me then, I might have crumbled. But he didn't. He stepped back from me, then moved toward the couch. "I'll help you carry this stuff." He picked up an armload of sheets and coverlets; I hugged the pillows to my chest. We trudged glumly to Dotty's house.

I deposited the bedding in Dotty's room while Tyler reclaimed crowbar, hammer and chisel from the hall. With those and the items he'd brought, we went to the study where I showed him the place I thought the door was stuck. He lay on his stomach, using his phone for light. Grumbling about not seeing well enough, he took pictures under the bookcase and then went to the desk to study them. I noticed he hesitated before sitting in Thomas' chair.

"It's all right," I said. "Thomas is on our side."

Tyler flashed an abashed smile, and sat. I perched on the desk, idly flipping through the book on symbols. I hadn't researched the words *key* or *garden*. Would the book have any clues?

Nothing on *key* except St. Peter, but *garden* was an eye-opener. "Tyler, what was the inscription on the bookcase in town? The one in Sam's antique shop."

He looked up. "Uh, SoS 4:12. Why?"

"Eureka!" I cried. "SoS means Song of Solomon. The numbers would be chapter 4, verse 12. 'A garden enclosed is my sister, my spouse; a spring shut up, a fountain sealed.'

"Well, that's clear as mud." He tapped his phone. "There are three wheels on the right-hand bookcase. I think the middle wheel is caught in the track, around four feet from center."

"About where my pencil stopped when I probed with it." I was still intrigued with the Bible verse, but Tyler went to use the crowbar on the bookcase, lying down to reach in and pull. He grunted; metal squealed. He called me over.

"Hold the phone for me, Meg. I'm going to try some WD-40. It's just so hard to see through a gap two inches from the floor."

"Well, sit up when you spray. Don't breathe the fumes."

"Yes, Mother."

I mock-punched his arm, relieved we'd moved away from the earlier awkwardness. It was a damned-if-you-do and damned-if-you-don't situation. My brain said one thing; my body, another. Neither was happy.

Unexpectedly, Tyler put down the tools and sat cross-legged facing me. He asked, "Do you *want* to go back to Florida?"

"No. It's financial necessity." I took a deep breath, readying myself to explain what happened. "I earned a good salary in Chicago, but I spent every penny I didn't need to pay off my student loans. Got that done, I'm proud to say, yet after the divorce and move to Florida, I had very little left. I didn't apply for a Florida law license since I knew I wasn't going to stay. I've been working low-paying jobs, and still have a way to go before I can reach independent living."

"Okay," he said. "You're starting to make sense." Then he was back on task, spraying, prodding, and wiggling the crowbar. He picked up the chisel and mallet to scrape at the floor under the bookcase. "Might not be the wood. Could be a track joint's loose." He applied hands and tools with full concentration.

I felt absurdly pleased he hadn't quite given up on me, that he was trying to find an answer to the long-distance issue. It was charming—but wishful thinking on his part. I pushed thoughts of miraculous solutions out of my mind.

While I aimed the phone light where he directed, the Bible verse nagged at me. Sure, the words made an obvious case for virginity, but why were they referenced on a bookshelf in Maine?

A spring shut up, a fountain sealed. What did that mean? I moved Tyler's phone away from the bookcase to consult AI on biblical times and gardens. I read how gardens were places with abundant water.

"Oh! Ohmygod. Tyler! It's the cistern. That's where water is shut up, sealed."

"What are you talking about?" He frowned, looking annoyed I'd interrupted his efforts. "Move the phone back. I need the light."

"In Thomas' letter, he mentioned a key and a garden. There's a key to something by the cistern in the cellar. Maybe it's where we find treasure."

Tyler turned, propped himself up on an arm, and took the phone from my hand. "After all this work to get into the Secret Room, you want to give up and check the cellar? No. One thing at a time. I'm ready to test these doors. Go to the desk and do your magic."

I was on my way to adjust the drawers when Tyler's phone pinged. He sat up, answered, and cried, "*What?* No! Is he all right? How bad?" A pause to listen, then, "Okay, okay thanks…thanks for calling."

He clicked off, stood up, and said, "Rik's in the hospital. By the buoy shack, he was struck in the forehead by someone hiding around the corner of the building. Docs are checking him out. He told a deputy to let me know the stone is gone."

13.

"Oh, no! Poor Erik. Was it bad?"

"The deputy didn't sound concerned," Tyler said.

"I'll text Erik to say we're sorry he was injured and not to worry about the stone."

Tyler strode across the study to Thomas' desk, where I was starting the text. He waved his phone at me. "What do you mean 'not to worry'? The stone was our only lead for finding Dotty. We were supposed to get some answers tonight, but Rik blew it."

"That's cold," I said.

"You were the one who insisted he place the stone. I wasn't good enough. Then Rik pulls a rookie move, and we're back to square one!"

"Do I detect a note of jealousy?"

"No." Tyler nodded vigorously.

I smiled at the tell of a lie. "Ty, I thought Erik had training for this sort of thing. I didn't want you hurt."

"Oh? Oh." Sounding calmer, he said, "I'm still angry we lost the stone."

"It's gone, so no point making Erik feel bad," I reasoned. "I just wish we knew what was so important about a rock."

Just then, in one of those weird coincidences, my brother called. "Megs, you will never guess how important the stone is," Mark said. "We could get into the history books!"

"Wait. Let me put you on speaker so Tyler can hear, too." I

motioned him closer, and he perched on the edge of the desk. "Okay. Go on."

"I thought the letters looked Slavic, so I went looking for someone in the Slavic department, but it was empty—it's Saturday. I found a teaching assistant in the Scandinavian languages office. He also spoke Russian, so I showed him the picture and told him the stone was from Maine. I swear, if he hadn't been sitting, he'd have fallen down. He grabbed my phone, scrutinized it, and asked if I had photos of making the find or witnesses. I said no, and he deflated like a balloon. 'People will never believe it, then. They'll say the stone came from elsewhere.'

"He said it was a Norse inscription, specifically Younger Futhark runes, used during the Viking age. There was only one word: ᛖᛁᚱᛁᚴᚱ, which means Erik."

"Erik, like Erik the Red?" Tyler asked.

"I thought of him, too, but the T.A. said Erik the Red never made it to North America. His son, Leif Eriksson, got as far as Canada. There's no undisputed evidence any Norse explorer went south into what's now the U.S.

"The T.A. didn't realize we can identify rock origins by their composition. If I find the stone and others from Spear Point are identical, we have good evidence the stone was inscribed there. I can't wait to do petrographic analysis on that stone."

Mark sounded so happy and excited, I hated to tell him, "Uh, we lost the stone."

"WHAT?"

After he heard about the theft, he swore, then went silent. I gave him a moment to mourn his lost fame before saying if we found the stone, he'd be the first to know. He clicked off after a dispirited goodbye.

I looked at Tyler; he looked at me. "Colin," he said. "It has to be Colin who wanted the stone. A find like that would make his career."

"But would he bash Erik to get it?"

"Desperate people do desperate things."

"Why not just ask Erik for it? Or ask you."

Tyler shook his head. "I don't know. I'm a simple guy: go to work, pay my bills, don't drink and drive. All of this cloak and dagger stuff is beyond me."

"I hear you, but you've invited Colin to Spear Point for the Secret Room opening. I don't think that's a good idea."

"Hmm…." Tyler pushed off the edge of the desk to pace. "What if…what if he wants to put the stone back in place? I'm pretty sure I told him Mark found it by the grotto. A visit here is the perfect opportunity for Colin to mosey over to the grotto and make the 'great find.'"

"We'd know he was lying, and more importantly, he'd be guilty of assault on a police officer. That's a felony in most jurisdictions."

Tyler rubbed the back of his neck. "He sounded so sincere when he denied knowing anything about the note. I had to remind him the stone had been in Dotty's parlor. Then Colin said, 'Oh, yeah. I remember that one. Had graffiti on it, right?'"

"*Ancient* graffiti," I mused. "But weren't people illiterate back then? Must have been unusual to know how to write your name. Or someone else's name—like an homage. Maybe old Leif Eriksson cited his dad."

"Sounds like fantasy to me," Tyler said. "How 'bout we stick to what we know? Let's get those doors open."

He went to the bookcases while I set the drawers to engage the Secret Room motor, but the doors only moved a few inches apart—too narrow a space to fit through. Tyler went to the gap, thrust his arm inside, and took pictures. With the motor noises growling, I told Tyler to back away before I shut the door.

He said, “This day just gets better and better.”

We studied the pictures. To the south, the dim light seemed to reveal a file cabinet, desk, desk chair, lamp, and a chest on slender legs.

“What’s that?” Tyler wondered.

“Looks like a jewelry armoire.” To his puzzled expression, I said, “A standing jewelry box.”

“Dotty’s stuff,” he concluded. “And there’s nothing to the north, at least, nothing we can see without more light. I’ll run over to the shed, get a shop light and tactical flashlight. If nothing else works, I’ll take a crowbar to those damned doors.”

“Tomorrow,” I said wearily. “We’ve both lost patience today. We don’t want to wreck the place, so let’s knock off. Oh, we could take down the last of the books and the shelves to lighten the load, and then call it a night.”

Tyler agreed, so we cleared the bookcases. Looking around at the mess in the room, I was glad Dotty couldn’t see what we’d done to her house. Still, I’d happily listen to her strongest rebuke if only she were here.

I thought of texting Erik to let him know what we’d learned about the stone but knew I shouldn’t disturb him; he’d need rest. And, fearing I’d get Tyler’s hackles up again, I didn’t mention Erik when I walked Tyler to the door.

“You’re sure you want to stay here?” he asked.

I shrugged helplessly. The kiss that followed was better than I’d imagined as a teen: intense, passionate, filled with promise. When we came up for air, my knees were weak. Tyler smiled—not the practiced smile he used to dazzle, but one I’d never seen and liked better. He smiled with his eyes, authentic and happy. I stared after him when he stepped outside, and then shut the front door, leaning against it for support.

Why was I being such a prude? My shoulder angel assured me I was protecting myself from heartbreak. The shoulder devil gave me a sour side-eye and stalked off.

My dreams were frustrating and exhausting. I kept trying to do something, always to meet an obstacle and fail. When my phone buzzed, waking me, I felt relief.

"Erik! I'm so glad you called. How are you?"

"Not bad. Got a big ole bruise on my forehead, but otherwise, okay. Good thing I have a hard head."

I tried to ask more about what happened, but Erik hedged and said he'd rather not go into it. Then he surprised me by saying he still wanted to keep our 'non-date' for a meal together. I felt too guilty about his injury to beg off.

"I'll have to buy something and bring it out to Spear Point," he said. "I'm not up for a restaurant outing."

"Don't bother. Do you like shepherd's pie? I have the ingredients to make one."

"Sounds good, but I promised you a fancy meal."

"Tell you what: I'll dress up and set a nice table. We'll pretend it's fine dining."

Erik chuckled. "Okay, but I don't want to give you a lot of work." He paused. "How about a picnic? Haven't been picnicking in years."

"You're on. Oh, and maybe you can drive out with Colin. Tyler invited him to view the opening of the Secret Room."

"Actually, Colin's asked to borrow my boat. His date last night went really well, he said. They planned another date today. Colin thought a boat ride would impress her. They're going to stop at Spear Point, then go on. I can hitch a ride out there if Ty will drive me home."

"You must trust Colin a lot to lend him your boat," I observed.

"Not a problem. He's better at boat handling than I am."

I just had to tell Erik about what my brother learned and our suspicions Colin stole the stone. Erik was astounded by the stone's inscription—"Hey, that's my name!"—but he refused to believe Colin took it. "No way. Colin never wants to see the inside of a cell again. He can't be the one."

Was he right, or blinded by friendship? I decided to let things play out, but was glad to have police presence, even if Erik hadn't distinguished himself yesterday.

We firmed up the plans. The boat would arrive around noon. He'd bring drinks and dessert.

I'd make two batches of pie, plus salad and spoon bread. Tyler, Colin and his date could eat at Tyler's; Erik and I would picnic by the grotto, keeping watch in case Colin decided to sneak out there to replace the stone.

After the call, I put on yesterday's clothes and dashed to Tyler's cottage, hoping I wouldn't wake him. He answered the door looking so adorably sleep tousled, I forgot why I stood on his doorstep.

"Meg?" he prompted.

"Uh, yeah, good morning. Um, do you have hamburger?"

He peered at me. "You're making hamburgers for breakfast?"

"No, I..." I stepped into his living room and explained the plot I'd hatched with Erik. "The only thing I'm worried about," I confessed, "is if Colin has a gun."

"Not Colin. He and his cousin played with a gun when they were kids. The cousin shot himself. He recovered, but Colin was traumatized, hates guns. And besides, who brings a gun on a date?"

I had to admit the idea was far-fetched, but nothing this week made sense: Dotty's disappearance, Colin trying to get into the Secret Room, Chloe turning up, a demand for a stone with historic significance, the attack on Erik. At this point, I trusted no one but Tyler and my family.

Back at Dotty's, I found an unopened bottle of Worcestershire sauce in the pantry, then went to the cellar for potatoes, onion, and home-canned corn and peas—feeling no dread down there at all. In the garden, I picked garlic, buttercrunch lettuce, tomatoes, radishes and herbs, so I had what I needed for the main dish. The spoon bread ingredients came from the cupboard except for the eggs. I still had the carton Tyler bought for me at the General Store.

Tyler arrived with equipment to tackle the Secret Room. I showed him how to work the desk drawers, and then left him to it.

When I got the glass pans in the oven, I checked my phone and still had time for a quick shower and dip into Dotty's fabulous wardrobe. I selected a white voile dress with embroidered white roses banding neck, waist, and hem above a deep ruffle. Insertion lace and pin tucks filled sleeves, bodice and skirt.

Though I chose not to try a corset, my ordinary underwear was well hidden beneath a corset cover and petticoat. On impulse, I wrapped a lacy shawl over my shoulders and tied it in front. I wouldn't quite pass for an Edwardian lady since I left my hair down, wore no hat or gloves, and was stuck with completely inappropriate sandals. Still, I liked what I saw in the beveled-glass mirror inside the wardrobe's door. I stopped admiring myself when I remembered my pie and bread. Sprinting to the kitchen, I pulled my dishes from the oven and turned it off.

The air muggy from yesterday's rain, and now, the heat from the oven made the room oppressively hot. I opened windows and the door to the screen porch, then left for the cooler territory of the study.

Tyler was seated at the desk, peering at his phone. When I entered, he looked up and his face lit, then it dimmed.

I recoiled, asking, "What?"

"Sorry. For a moment there, I thought you were Dotty."

"But it was just little, old me," I said with mock chagrin.

"Yeah," he said, continuing the tease. Then his tone changed. "C'mere. You've got to see this." He tapped his phone.

I went to stand behind the chair. Laying my hand on Tyler's left shoulder, I peered over his right. His delicious lips just inches away, my thoughts were on him rather than the screen as he reset a video. He interrupted my reverie by saying, "I took this inside the Secret Room. Finally had good light to scan the east wall and the north end. Here. Watch."

The video started with a dark, blank wall, moving on to the end and turning the corner where an empty gun rack stood. As the camera scanned left, there was a sharp, bright flash leaving an after image of a figure in white. A second or two later, the figure faded and winked out.

I gasped. "Was that…was that our ghostly Amanda?"

"Doubtful." Tyler sat back in the chair so I had to move away. "Optical illusion. My shop light bulb popped, producing the flare. Then the flashlight batteries gave out. Maybe all the dampness damaged them. Who knows?"

"It looks just like a woman in white. Unbelievable. We should post the video to some online paranormal site."

I shook my head, and then I saw it. "Eww! Mouse droppings on the desk." I pointed to Tyler's right. There could be no other explanation for black pellets shaped like rice. I followed the trail to the west wall, where I saw a hole in the floor molding.

Tyler said, “Meg, your dress isn’t buttoned.”

“Oh.” I reached around my back to find bare skin. “Uh, can you…?”

“Sure.” He came to where I was standing, made a little circle with his hand signaling me to turn, and started on the buttons. I felt tingly all over. “Okay. Got it done.” Looking down, he added. “I’ll bring in some steel wool for the mouse hole. Should stop them.”

Just then, his phone pinged. He went back to the desk. “They’re here. I’ll go out and help them tie up in the boathouse.”

“I forgot the picnic basket. Need to get it,” I told his departing back. After a few calming breaths, I headed toward the cellar.

A chill breeze in the back hall surprised me, but I knew what it meant. Weather was changing; there’d be fog rolling in. I couldn’t see it now, but I’d seen it before. It looked like a white tsunami, and it moved fast. Power boats raced for shore. Sailboats trimmed their sails and did the same.

Glad I’d added the shawl to my outfit, I approached the cellar steps when I heard shouting outside. Tyler: “Chloe! What the hell?” Colin: “Claire? What’s going on?” Tyler: “Her name’s Chloe, not Claire.” Erik: “Chloe, put down the gun.”

Thoughts flooded my brain. *Get a kitchen knife. No. A knife’s no match for a gun. Go to the cellar and hide. She won’t know I’m there. Better to be a hidden asset than another hostage.* In the end, I grabbed a knife and ran down the cellar steps, leaving the light off but the door open so I could hear what was going on above.

I heard the screen porch door creak, and Chloe say, “Move!” Feet shuffling in the kitchen, and Chloe, again. “Over there. All of you. Other side of the room.”

“What do you want?” Tyler asked.

"Why, you, darling. We're going to spend some time together in a little place I rented on an island. No one to bother us. That's what we need. Time to become the soulmates we truly are." In a different tone, she asked, "Where's the woman who's supposed to be here? The one Erik wants to see."

"Went to Hopewell this morning to meet her parents. Took my car," Tyler lied.

Good. He's covering for me.

"She stood me up?" Erik asked.

"Must not be that into you," Tyler said, and I thought I heard a hint of a smirk in his tone.

"This food's still warm," Chloe countered.

"She made it before she left. I put it in the oven," Tyler said.

"Oh! A man who can cook. We're going to have such a good time together! But no shepherd's pie. Uck. Can't stand the stuff."

I moved, slowly, carefully, to the space behind the cistern, thinking what to do next. I could sneak out through the bulkhead—no. Tyler chained it shut. I could…well, there wasn't anything to do but wait.

"Claire, I don't understand," Colin said. "I thought…I thought we had something going."

"The name's Chloe, you sweet man. You've been nice to me, but I'm destined for Tyler. 'Fraid I had to use you to get to him, so now, it's goodbye."

Erik said, "You can't leave in the boat. Fog's moving in. And there's no other way off Spear Point at high tide."

"What's the big deal about a little fog?"

"A boat would hit the shoals and sink. If the cold water doesn't get you, the sharks will," Colin said.

"Sharks?"

"Yeah. The ones with big teeth—great whites."

"I don't care! My Tyler will get us through," Chloe gushed.

"*Tyler?*" Colin and Erik snickered.

"Not me," he said. "I can't drive a boat. Never had one, never taken the wheel. I don't even know how to back out of the boathouse."

Silence. Then I heard her say, "Drop your phones and kick them toward me. That's it. Got 'em. So…we're going to wait in the boathouse until the fog goes away. The second it lifts, we leave. You, Erik, can drive the boat?"

He must have nodded because Chloe went on. "This place have a basement?"

"Yes. It's there," Colin said.

"Then, dear Colin, into the basement with you. I can't have three men on the boat, but two's okay. I can watch two. Oh, but don't worry. I don't want to harm you. Not unless I really have to. But him—this Erik guy—I don't care about him. If any of you try to stop us from leaving, I'll shoot him. So, Colin, trot on down those stairs."

He came to the door and started down the steps. Before he reached the last one, I heard, "You two move that thingy to block the door."

"The wringer washer?" Tyler asked.

"Yes. It looks heavy. Now tie up the doorknob with clothesline and wrap it around the thingy."

With the door closed and the washer in place, I heard no more. Colin stood in the dark at the foot of the stairs.

Great. I was locked in the cellar with the man crazy enough to mug a cop while Tyler and Erik were held at gunpoint by a madwoman.

14.

I uncoiled from my crouch behind the cistern. "Colin," I hissed.

He jumped backward and yelped.

With eyes new to dim light, Colin must have seen a white shape coming out of the cistern. To his credit, he didn't scream. I would have.

"What's going on down there?" Chloe shouted through the door. I froze, fearful she'd open it until I remembered she couldn't move the barricade without help.

Colin yelled, "Just stepped on something." To me, he whispered, "Who're you?"

"Megan Fields, Dotty Hartley's great-niece."

"You're not in Hopewell."

"Obviously. Go turn on the light. Top of the stairs." When he hesitated, I said, "Chloe knows you're down here."

I was itching to ask him if he stole the stone and attacked Erik, but I held my tongue. What if he said yes? Better to play dumb.

At the top of the stairs, Colin flipped the light switch. I blinked at the sudden brightness. After he tried to muscle the door open, he came down rubbing his shoulder. Next, he pulled the bolt on the bulkhead doors and pushed, reacting with surprise when they didn't budge.

"Tyler chained the bulkhead from the outside," I said, "after you hid down here."

Colin grimaced. "Where's your phone?"

"In my bedroom. I left it there when I changed clothes."

"We'll have to break out of here." He checked Dotty's garden tools, grumbling when he didn't find picks or sledgehammers, eventually settling on a shovel.

I watched him pace near the walls but didn't hold out much hope a shovel could dislodge the stone foundation, which filled the bottom four feet of the room. Wood above might give way with some heavy pounding. I suggested this to Colin.

"Nah. Old wood's hard. This shovel's pretty light. But…" He passed me to peer at a spot across from the back corner of the cistern. "What's this hatch for?"

"Hatch?" I moved closer. Sure enough, there was a hinged, wood panel roughly three-foot square embedded in the wall about six feet above the floor. Four slats ran vertical, not horizontal, like the walls. I never noticed it before, probably because I'd been afraid of the cellar.

"What's on the other side of this wall?" Colin asked.

"Uh…." I had to think about what was next to the laundry room door. "Stairs to the second floor."

"So, this is a cubby under the stairs. Why's it locked? There's a keyhole."

"Wow. Hard to see. I'm amazed you spotted it."

He grinned. "Finding things is what I do. Now, we need a key."

Key… Just last night, I'd deciphered Thomas' note about a key, garden and treasure. Discovering that garden meant abundant water in biblical times, I intended to explore the cistern, but got distracted by Tyler and the Secret Room doors.

I told Colin, "It's in the cistern somewhere."

He shook his head. "Wouldn't be inside. These things store rain water. No one would risk a loose brick in a water tank. Let's look at the stones nearby. I'll take this wall; you take the back one." He began probing the wall he'd chosen.

I was getting annoyed with Colin. It wasn't just his giving me orders: He'd thought of things I hadn't. But when he found a stone with almost no mortar, I had to admit he *was* good at finding things.

"It's in there tight," he said. "I need something thin to fit between the stones."

I reached to the floor for the kitchen knife and handed it to him. He looked up. "You were planning to stab someone?"

"To defend myself, yes."

"Good. I like a woman who can make tough decisions. Had to make a few of those myself."

Was he talking about assaulting Erik? Not the time to ask while he held the knife.

Colin pried with the knife point and twisted the stone. A brass skeleton key lay in a niche on its back. "All right!" he crowed. He used the key on the hatch, then pulled open the panel. "We're in, but I'll need a ladder to get up there. Here's the knife: put it somewhere safe, and see if there's a step stool around."

"Yes, Sir!" I said smartly.

"Sorry. I'm used to young volunteers. They leave stuff everywhere. Please get a ladder."

Mollified, I found what he wanted by Dotty's tools. Colin climbed up to the hatch in the wall, sat on the edge, hauled his legs through the gap, and slid in.

I stood just beneath the hatch. "What do you see?"

"Underside of stairs. Cobwebs. Dust. I have to hunch down, but there's room to move around. I see one small light to my left."

"Could be the mousehole. The study's in front of you."

"Finally caught a break," Colin said. "Plaster's thin in there, probably because bookcases would cover the walls. Contractors took shortcuts even back in the day."

"How do you know about the plaster?"

"I checked the study for hidden panels when I, uh, let myself into the house. Pass me the shovel—no, wait. I see something in the corner. It's roundish, dark." His footsteps moved right. "It's a kettle. A big, cast-iron kettle with a handle. YES! I *knew* it was here. Must be Hiram Miller's kettle, his pirate treasure!" I heard the clink of coins passing through Colin's fingers. "Get something to put the treasure in."

"Don't waste time on that now," I said.

"Have to. I need the kettle for a wrecking ball."

"Oh, I don't know…." I cringed at the image of Dotty finding a hole in the study before realizing she wouldn't give a second thought to walls when Tyler was in danger.

"We're running out of time. If the fog lifts, Erik and Tyler will be gone," Colin said.

I edged backward from the cistern, found the picnic basket, and hurried to reach it up and through the hatch to Colin. Coins pattered onto wicker, and the basket was back. I took it as Colin said, "Move away from the wall. I'm going to swing the kettle. Could hit the back wall by accident."

From my new position at the end of the cistern, I took a quick look at the coins, which were black and green. No gold, just silver and copper, I guessed. Not many—around a dozen.

I heard heavy thuds on the walls as Colin warmed up his swing, and then lath shattering and a rain of chunks. "I'm through!" he cried. "I'll get you out in a minute."

Less than a minute later, I heard grunting and scraping on wood at the top of the stairs. As I mounted the steps, the door opened. Colin held scissors and severed clothesline in his hands. He said, "Go call 911. Tell them Detective Erik Lundgren may be killed if they delay, then mention Tyler. They'll move faster if it's one of their own."

I set down the basket of coins and went for my phone, making the call and giving details in a frenzied rush. The dispatcher told me to slow down. After I repeated my words, she said she'd send officers immediately.

"But it'll still take nearly half an hour," I told Colin when I rejoined him in the kitchen. "There's the drive from Brunswick, getting the Fire & Rescue boat in Hopewell, and motoring out here. Oh! What about the fog?"

"Not a problem," Colin said. "They have a depth gauge and GPS charting. Erik's boat has those, too. Good thing Claire—I mean, Chloe—knows squat about boats, or she'd have gotten away by now."

"Really?"

Colin smirked. He looked out the windows. "Fog's thick. Easy to get to the boathouse without being seen."

"Why not wait for the police?"

"They could spook her, make her start shooting. No, we have to get control of her before they arrive. I can sneak around to the boat doors and tackle Chloe, but she has to be looking toward the door at the top of the stairs or she'll see me. She's probably on the dock holding the guys in the boat, facing them. I need a distraction."

"What if I go with you, stay by the entrance door, and yell or something?"

"Might work or might not. Threatened, she could focus on her captives."

I sighed, looked down, and noticed what I was wearing. An idea blossomed even as I said, "I can be the Woman in White, a ghost." I pulled my lace scarf over my head.

"You just look like a woman wearing white," Colin said.

"Okay…." I pursed my lips, and thought some more. Then, I had it. I went to the pantry and pulled out the flour canister. Setting it on the table, I took a handful and dusted my face.

"Better. Cover your hands, too."

"Not yet." I remembered Dotty's antique flashlight in the drawer. I grabbed it, pressed the button, and hid the tube between my hands, aiming the light upward toward my chin. This time, when I faced Colin, he did a doubletake. "Silver eyes? How do you do that?"

"Trick of the light," I said, shutting off the flashlight before dousing my hands with flour. I took a deep breath. "Ready?"

He looped the rope over his arm, put the scissors in his back pocket. "Ready."

Small chance we could be seen from the boathouse. There were no windows on the side facing us except for glass in the door. And the fog was dense enough to limit vision to less than ten feet. We picked our steps carefully so as not to crunch gravel or slip on damp rocks.

When we reached the boathouse door, Colin gestured he was going around to the lower area with the boat doors. He held up five fingers; I mouthed 'Five minutes?' He nodded before he stole away. I crouched by the door wall, waiting for what I hoped was the right amount of time by counting Mississippis.

I remembered Tyler's childhood nickname for me—Scaredy Cat. Just now, it fit. My hands shook. My heart beat wildly. What if I failed, screwed up, and someone died?

Focus. Focus on Tyler. Just do it.

Holding my left hand in a death grip on the light, I threw open the door. The fog swirled, wrapping me in a cocoon. Suddenly, I felt safe, unafraid. My right hand shot out, pointing at a barely visible Chloe watching me from the dock.

Words boomed from my mouth, words in a voice that didn't sound like me. "Release him! Release my child!"

Chloe screamed and leveled her gun at me.

I dove away from the door. Fear engulfed me. I felt clammy and hot at the same time. Below, I heard yelling, thumps and scuffling, a gunshot and a cry of pain.

No! Not Tyler. Not my Tyler. My chest seized up. I couldn't breathe.

"Meg? You all right?" Tyler's voice.

I gulped in air. "Yes. Fine."

"Come down here. We have Chloe, but Erik's hurt."

I picked myself up and descended to dock level. Erik was closest. He sat huddled against a post, knees up, right hand clutching his left shoulder. Blood soaked his windbreaker sleeve. Chloe's gun and the remains of a cut zip tie lay by his left thigh.

About six feet away, Chloe sprawled on her stomach with Tyler sitting on her lower back, pinning her with his weight as he tied her hands with clothesline. Colin concentrated on binding her ankles. Chloe vacillated between insults, pleading and whining.

I knelt by Erik. "What can I do?"

"Get a towel from the boat. Should be one in the cabin."

Erik's boat rocked gently in the slip. I found the towel, and hurried back to Erik. Holding the towel against his bleeding arm, I asked, "What happened?"

"Colin tackled Chloe, took her down, but she still had the gun. It was aimed at Tyler. I jumped out of the boat to go for the gun and she fired. Grazed my shoulder." He flinched, then managed a weak smile. "Know how they say on TV shows 'It's only a flesh wound.'? What they don't say is it hurts like hell."

"I'm so sorry," I said, patting his hand.

Tyler sat beside the now securely tied Chloe. He spoke to her in a conversational tone. "The few times I've seen you, you did all the talking. It's my turn. Wanna know who I really am? Listen up.

"I lied on the dating profile, put down what I thought women would like. Truth is I detest flavored coffee, rom-coms, and craft fairs. Don't make my bed, drink out of the o.j. carton, leave my clothes all over the floor Sound like your soulmate?"

"I…don't…know," Chloe said.

"I'm not some plastic guy from a romance movie who'll shower you with attention. I work long hours. I belch. I fart. I cut my toenails in the living room. This your Prince Charming?"

"Eww, no." Chloe's face twisted with disgust. If she could have shrunk away from him, I'm sure she would have, but lying on her side trussed up like a Thanksgiving turkey, all she could do was scowl.

Tyler wasn't done. "When you get out of jail—" He looked over his shoulder toward me. "She is going to jail, isn't she?"

"Definitely. Four counts of criminal restraint, two counts of attempted kidnapping, attempted grand theft, aggravated assault of a police officer and/or attempted murder, depending on the prosecution's strategy. She'll do time."

Chloe started in with noisy weeping. Tyler ignored her and went on. "Forget about me. I don't want you; I never did, never will. Nothing can change my mind. And I'm done with online dating. Someone real in your life is so much better." He smiled at me.

The crying stopped abruptly. Chloe raised her head. "The fake ghost? She's that bitchy lawyer, isn't she?"

"Watch your mouth." Tyler left her, and came to join Erik and me.

"Is it possible she has Dotty?" I whispered.

"No. If she had leverage on me, she wouldn't need a gun."

"And your confession—is it true?"

"I made some of it up. Won't tell you which parts."

"Gratitude. But…."

"Oh, you mean *that* part. That's true. I don't lie about important things."

It felt like my smile spread from ear to ear. My eyes misted.

Tyler ran a fingertip down my cheek. "Meg…."

"Yes??"

"What is this gunk on your face? Man, you look awful."

"Oh, you charmer," I said. "It's flour."

Erik groaned. "So, you two are a thing? You could've told me. But right now, all I want to know is when will the damned rescue boat get here?"

I looked to the boat doors. "Not long. It's been at least twenty minutes. Just a few minutes more."

"Help me stand," Erik said. "Back's killing me in this slump."

I stood in front as a sort of spotter in case Erik teetered forward. Tyler took a firm hold of Erik's waist. Erik lifted his torso and pulled his legs under him. He stood shakily, wincing.

Something fell from Erik's windbreaker pocket. I picked it up. Tilting my head, frowning, I waved the runestone at him. "Why do you have this? You said it was stolen."

15.

"Where's Dotty?" Tyler demanded with murderous intensity. If Erik hadn't been holding his bleeding arm, I'm sure Tyler would have grabbed him by the throat.

"I don't know," Erik cried. "I don't know anything about Mrs. Hartley." He turned to face Colin. "Keep an eye on the woman, okay? I need to caucus with these two."

"*Caucus*? Fancy," Colin replied. He left his spot by the boat doors to stand over Chloe, who glared at everyone in stony silence.

Erik, Tyler and I moved closer to the stairs. "Don't want her listening in," Erik began in a low, soft voice. "I took the stone for my father. He always believed the Norse—our ancestors—found Maine before other Europeans. Used to drive my mother crazy how much money he donated to the Norwegian Heritage Society, hoping someone would come up with proof.

"I didn't pay attention to his cause—I mean, who cares? Then he developed Alzheimer's. We got bad news from the doc this week: his decline is accelerating. He—"

Erik squeezed his eyelids shut, took a deep breath and blinked rapidly when he opened watery eyes. "He's my *dad*. And he's not gonna be himself for long. I had to do something to show him…to…to—"

"I get it," Tyler said, "and I'm truly sorry about your father. But, why not ask for the stone it? Why send a ransom note?"

"Not a ransom note. I made no promises or threats."

Tyler looked at me. I nodded. "Legally, he's correct."

"Still doesn't answer why you didn't come to me for the stone," Tyler said.

"With Mrs. Hartley missing, I didn't think you'd have time for my problems, and time is running out."

"We'd have helped," I said.

"I couldn't be sure of that or about the stone. Maybe I was wrong, and the stone wasn't Norse. Had to see it again. And I figured, after all this time, someone must have told Mrs. Hartley it was important. She'd store it in the Secret Room. I had to find the paper with instructions for the door."

"You knew about Thomas' letter? How?" Tyler asked.

"Once, when I was visiting you, I saw Mrs. Hartley in the kitchen studying a piece of paper. I asked what she was doing. She said she was rereading a letter from her husband with a puzzle about a secret place. I offered to help because I was good at puzzles. She smiled—I must have been all of eight—and informed me she'd solved the puzzle except for one little bit. Then she folded the letter, put it in a book, and said if I hurried to take the book back to the study, she'd give me a treat. I ran both ways to get my reward—a red velvet cupcake with cream cheese icing. Still remember how good it was."

"You," Tyler said, "broke into the library looking for the paper."

"Correction: I thought I saw an intruder and went in to check."

I smirked. "And did you find this intruder in the book boxes?"

"False alarm," Erik said with a crooked smile.

"That's your story?" Tyler asked.

Erik nodded. "And I'm sticking to it."

"But wait a minute. Who ambushed you by the buoy shack?" I asked.

"No one. I tripped and fell. Hit my head. I was too embarrassed to tell the guys at the station."

"Oh, really," I scoffed. "We're supposed to believe that? It's more likely you staged the whole thing."

Tyler gave me a meaningful side eye. "I told you he was tricky."

Erik shrugged. "Since I had the stone in my pocket, I showed it to Dad. He was so happy. I'll hang onto the memory through what's to come."

Tyler said, "You raised our hopes about finding Dotty, but you saved my life today and got shot. I won't rat on you. Still, I think you should tell your captain about the shack, so deputies can stop looking for a criminal who doesn't exist."

"You're right," Erik agreed.

"One more thing," I said. "What were you planning to do with the stone?"

"Bring it back here and lead Colin to it. That way, his Viking expedition would be a success. You'd better take it," he told Tyler, who slipped the stone into his back pocket.

"Now, it's a double success with the pirate treasure, and all," I mused.

Erik and Tyler stared at me. Both of them said, "What treasure?"

Colin called, "Hey guys, the boat's here. They've anchored and launched the dinghy." He shook his head. "Wish I had my phone to call them." He scowled at Chloe. "She threw our phones in the water."

Chloe cried, "Ha!"

"Ha, yourself," I said, sounding juvenile even to myself. "You're going to jail."

Chloe made doe eyes at Tyler. "You're not really going to have me arrested, are you? You know there's a connection between us."

Tyler groaned. "Get this straight: No connection. No nothing! I never want to see you again."

She must have decided Colin would be a soft touch. Turning to him, she said, "Tyler's been so mean to me, but you've been good, Colin. You and I—"

He rounded on her, pointing a finger. "You lied to me, locked me in the cellar, tried to kidnap my friends and steal a boat. You shot Erik," Colin reminded her. "There's no changing what you did." He turned toward the boat doors. "Dinghy's on its way. I'll go catch the bowline."

Two deputies and an EMT came ashore. One deputy looked at Chloe, then asked, "Detective Lundgren?"

"Her name's Chloe Goode—Goode with an e. She has a warrant for stalking, and she's facing other charges. Arrest her, Sullivan."

Chloe cried, "He's lying. These people tried to kidnap *me*. Just look at me. I'm tied up and they're free."

"Nice try," Colin sneered. He introduced himself to Deputy Sullivan, who arrested Chloe and recited her rights. Colin and the deputy worked to get Chloe, who whined shrilly about everything, out of the clothesline bonds and into handcuffs.

The EMT, a young woman, went directly to Erik. She had him sit on the stairs while she checked his vitals, cleaned the wound, and covering it with a bandage. Finished with Erik, she asked if anyone else were injured. We said we were fine.

The second officer, whose nametag read Deputy James, said, "Miss Fields?"

"Here." He eyed me skeptically, no doubt wondering why I looked like the undead. "I'm in disguise," I explained, though he didn't look reassured.

"You called this in. What happened here?"

I described what Chloe had done and how we all responded. Next, he interviewed Tyler, who added details about being held at gunpoint on the boat, Colin's Chloe take-down, and the shot hitting Erik.

The deputies had clearly heard enough. Deputy James asked the EMT if her patient could walk to the rescue boat. She said yes, so they made for the dinghy.

Once those two were aboard, Deputy James collected the gun in an evidence bag and instructed Tyler, Colin and me to come to the station to make formal statements as soon as we could. Colin said he'd return Erik's boat to its dock, then drive to the station. Tyler promised he and I would appear as soon as the tide let us leave Spear Point. Both deputies and Chloe went to the dinghy, which set off for the rescue boat.

"I need a drink," Colin said.

Tyler said, "Me, too. I've got some vodka, maybe some scotch, at the cottage. Megan?"

I shook my head. "I'm craving a shower and lunch. Anybody else hungry?"

We agreed to meet at the house in twenty minutes, which gave me time to reheat the shepherd's pie and scrub myself clean. As I changed into my own clothes, I studied Dotty's dress on the bed, sorry I'd given it such hard use and vowing to hand wash and iron it this evening.

When the men arrived, we all tucked into our food, saying nothing until we were sated. Then Colin showed Tyler the picnic basket with the coins from the pirate hoard. Tyler showed no surprise, so Colin must have told him about finding the kettle in the wall.

Tyler frowned. "I imagined gold and jewels; instead, there's nothing much here. I mean look at this one." He reached for a plain circle of tarnished silver. "It hardly looks like a coin. All it has is the letters NE on one side and XII on the other. Pretty dull."

Colin said, "Let's check it out. Megan, you have your phone?"

I photographed the coin and asked AI about it. The answer shocked me. "Tyler, what you're holding is one of the first coins minted in North America. It's a New England shilling from 1652. Only about forty of them were made in Boston."

"So, it's rare?" Tyler asked.

"Incredibly rare and valuable. A coin in good shape like this could be worth $200,000 to $400,000."

Colin whistled softly and peered into the basket. "I think you have three of them."

Tyler looked thunderstruck. My mouth fell open.

"A few of these others look interesting, too," Colin said. "This one says In Masathvsets—there's a v instead of a u—around the edge and has a picture of a drooping tree in the middle. The other side reads New England An Dom. In the center are the numbers 1652 and XII."

I took a picture and waited for the answer. "It's a 1652 Willow Tree Shilling. Only about 35 are left. It's worth at least as much as the other shillings. Could sell for a lot more."

We went through the rest of the coins, finding Dutch *daalders*, Spanish 4 *reales* and British copper farthings. Though some of these were lovely, they weren't particularly valuable.

"Well," Colin pushed away from the table, "this has been fun. You'd better put the hoard in a safe place. Did you ever get the Secret Room doors open?"

Tyler hung his head. "No."

"I guess it doesn't matter now. I feel gratified I predicted Hiram Miller found treasure, and here it is. Tomorrow, after I buy a phone, I'd like to come back to take pictures of the kettle *in situ* with the coins. Now, I better get Erik's boat back to Hopewell Harbor before low tide."

"Don't forget to go to the sheriff's station in Brunswick to make your statement," I said.

We walked Colin to the boathouse. The air was muggy but free of fog. I found Dotty's antique flashlight, which I'd dropped beside the door. Tyler helped Colin shove off from the dock. I noticed the runestone was still in Tyler's pocket.

When we were alone, I asked, "You didn't give Colin the stone. Why not?"

"We should think about the people who'd come to Spear Point if Colin published the find. All we need is a bunch of Viking wannabes in plastic-horned caps sneaking in at night for a drunken bonfire to honor Odin."

"Probably the only people who'd be interested are scholars," I reasoned.

"Don't bet on it. A lot of people might be curious, and we aren't equipped for crowds—no toilets, no trash collection, no security guards—and we have to buy our drinking water. Do we want to be hosting the multitude?"

"Can't we just tell Colin?"

"Maybe. Let's discuss the pros and cons on our way to the station in Brunswick. Tide should be low enough to cross the causeway in an hour. I just want to veg for a while, drink iced tea on the porch, and watch the waves to clear my head."

So, that's what we did, after slipping the coins and runestone through the narrow gap in the in Secret Room doors. Lounging in an Adirondack chair, Tyler took a sip of his tea. He turned to me. "You were brave today. What made you decide to impersonate a ghost?"

I shrugged. "It just came to me. I was terrified until I made my appearance at the boathouse and felt like I wasn't alone."

He tilted his head. "Your voice sounded different when you said,

'Release my child.' Why did you say those words?"

"Don't laugh, but I think Amanda was prompting me. You're her descendant—her child, so to speak. She wanted to protect you."

"Spooky," Tyler concluded. "This day's been so strange, I'll believe anything." He leaned forward in his chair and turned to me. "I'm not ashamed to admit I was scared out of my wits. I figured Chloe would kill Erik after he got us where we were going. She'd kill me, too, eventually, because I couldn't pretend to love her."

"Not even to save your life?"

"Like I said, I only lie about unimportant things."

"So, when you told her real life is better than anything online…."

"I wouldn't give up this moment for anything in cyberspace." He took my hand. "Meg, I don't want you to go to Florida."

"I don't either, but I can't see any alternative."

"Couldn't we stay in touch?"

"You know how long-distance relationships go."

"Hmm. Yeah. I had a college girlfriend take a job in Seattle. Wasn't supposed to be the end, but it was." Tyler looked at the sky. "I'd say it's around five. Can't tell for sure without my phone, but we should probably get going to the sheriff's department."

I remembered we planned to talk about the stone on the way. Was Tyler right that making it public would change our lives here? Was it our moral obligation to reveal the discovery? Was there some middle ground I hadn't thought of? What would Dotty say?

"I wish Dotty were here," I told Tyler as we walked to his car for the trip to Brunswick.

"I wish that every day, every moment."

We didn't talk much in the car. I couldn't bring myself to discuss the stone and what we should do. My brain needed a break from weighty decisions. Tyler must have felt the same way.

The station wasn't busy, so we made our statements without delay. We learned Erik didn't need hospitalization, so he'd gone home to rest. We didn't visit Chloe in the lockup.

"Well, that's that," Tyler said as we drove away. "Free, at last."

"Sounds good." I stretched my arms toward the windshield. I hadn't realized how tense I'd been until my shoulder muscles protested. All I had to do for the remainder of the day was make a late dinner and launder the clothing I'd borrowed from Dotty—simple, stress-free, homey things.

I turned to watch Tyler's profile, enjoying the sight, thinking how my opinion of him had reversed since I got to Spear Point. I smiled with pleasure.

The moment of serenity didn't last. As we crossed the causeway, I saw an unfamiliar car parked by Dotty's house. First, I was irked: Who was bothering us *now*? Then a stab of fear shot through me. Could it be a sheriff's deputy with bad news about Dotty?

No. A man and woman got out of the car, the man going round to open the trunk. My dad! Mom stood beside him, holding a hand to her brow, peering in our direction.

"It's my parents!"

We parked next to their rental car, and exchanged hugs all around. "Why didn't you tell us you were coming today?" I asked.

"I kept getting voicemail," Mom said. She took my measure. "You look good. This place agrees with you. And Tyler—" She paused to gaze at him, then said with a wry smile, "Well, you always look good."

"Glad you're here, Mrs. and Mr. Fields."

"Oh, for heaven's sake, call us Allison and Jason. You're not a child anymore."

He nodded, then offered to carry their bags. Dad gave him a

suitcase, but took the other himself.

Mom said, “There’s a car coming. Are you expecting someone?”

“No.” I turned toward the causeway. What I saw made me stare so hard, I’m sure my eyes bugged out.

Tooling along in the midnight-blue Lizzie with the top down were Dotty and a man in an old-fashioned motoring costume—a duster, I think it’s called. He had a dark cap and a pair of goggles to go along with the white coat. Dotty, in a high-necked white blouse, had her straw hat tied down by a red scarf. She waved with both hands. The man honked the horn, which made the classic *ahooga* sound.

The four of us stood on Dotty’s porch motionless as statues.

16.

Dotty's companion pulled the Lizzie up to the front steps, got out, and held open Dotty's door. A tall man with white hair, he trailed behind her as she mounted the stairs, arms out, crying, "My dears! I am so happy to see you all." Dotty went round the group touching cheeks and hands, smiling and murmuring greetings.

My mother was having none of this. She grabbed her aunt into a bear hug until Dotty protested, "Allison, I can't breathe." Mom pulled away, remarking stiffly, "Dotty, this isn't a family reunion. We're here because we feared something terrible happened to you. Five days! Five days without a word. Where were you?"

"I'll tell you everything inside," Dotty said. "But now, let me introduce Fred Mather, my first love." She beamed at the man, who removed his driving cap as she listed our names and relationships. He offered his hand all around.

Dotty asked Mom to show Fred to the parlor. "Must dash to the bathroom," she confessed. "An iced tea I drank in the car ran right through me." She turned to the door, frowning to find it locked.

"I have the key." Pulling it from my back pocket, I opened the door and followed Dotty to her bedroom. Better to take my licking now for using her room and clothing than wait for a scolding later.

Dotty glanced at the unmade bed and the disheveled dress laid on it. She said nothing until she returned from the bathroom and asked, "My dress fits you, and you like it?"

"Yes," I said, amazed by her response. I'd expected indignation, even anger.

"Marvelous! There's one problem solved." Dotty smiled as she led the way to the parlor.

Fred and my dad were seated on the sofa, listening to Tyler explain why the house had so little furniture. Fred rose when we entered; Dad did so tardily. He motioned Dotty to his place, then he eyed the room looking for another seat, but the two armchairs were taken. Mom had one and Tyler stood behind the other, holding it for me, I guessed. Wow. There's something about a Victorian setting that reminds us of proper manners.

Tyler saw my father's dilemma and went to the kitchen for a chair. While we waited for his return, no one spoke. We stared at each other, unsure what to say, until Mom expressed what was on all of our minds. "You put us through hell, imagining you'd been abducted, maybe tortured and killed. Why?"

Dotty nodded gravely. "I owe you all an apology. I am so, so sorry to have caused you distress. I'll never go away again without informing you. Can you forgive me?" She looked from face to face. I saw a mixture of incredulity and hesitation, prompting Dotty to go on.

"Believe me, I had no idea what would happen when I went to the cemetery to visit Thomas. All of a sudden, a parade of vintage cars began passing by. I moved to the curb for a better view, and what should I see but the Lizzie! I flagged down the driver, amazed to find it was Fred, who'd been *my* Fred, when I was fifteen and he, eighteen."

Dotty paused to look at him. "The brown hair's gone, but I'd know those big, deep, bedroom eyes anywhere." She smiled and then winked at Fred.

Returning her attention to the rest of us, Dotty continued her story. "Fred asked if I'd ride with him a way. I learned the Lizzie was restored in Oxford, then delivered to Brunswick, where Fred took charge of it. He agreed to drive it to Boston for his son-in-law, the actual owner. This was, in effect, the renewed Lizzie's maiden cruise.

"Well, as you can imagine, we had a lot to catch up on. We talked non-stop until we were nearly to Portland. Fred was ready to turn around and drive me home, but I didn't want to leave him. He was planning an overnight stay in New Hampshire at Wentworth by the Sea. The grand hotel was celebrating its 150th-year anniversary with candlelight dining, a costume ball, and fireworks.

"I decided to go there with him. They had period clothing available, so we could join in. I'd never traveled as far back as the 1870s; I was enchanted—*we* were enchanted. We stayed in that decade for several days." Dotty looked again toward Fred, who nodded. "Of course, we couldn't call anyone. Telephones hadn't been invented yet."

My mother rose to her feet. She stands 5'10" in her stocking feet, and she always wears heels. Glowering, arms crossed, no ancient goddess of wrath could have been more daunting. When she wagged her finger at Dotty, I shrank in my seat. Dotty looked up innocently. "Dorothy Ann Whitcomb Hartley, if you don't stop spouting nonsense about time travel , I'll have to believe you've lost your reason." She regarded Fred coldly. "Maybe you've been unduly influenced, or…or—"

Dotty cut in. "Jason, would you be so kind as to take Fred for a tour of Spear Point? He's never been here."

Dad said, "Uh, sure, but first, I'd like a closer look at the car's restoration job. Okay, Fred?" Fred, who seemed unruffled by my mother's hostility, exchanged a look with Dotty before he accompanied my dad outside.

"Now then," Dotty said, "I have not lost my reason; in fact, I've found it." She chuckled silently. "Truth is I've been privileged to live at Spear Point. It's a wonderful place, but it's lonely, and all I've done for years is think about the past. I couldn't see a positive future for myself."

Tyler said, "I've tried to be here for you."

"I know, dear. You've been good to me." She held up her hand to stop my mother's interruption, no doubt much the same as Tyler's reassurance. "What I've needed is someone who needs me. Someone to wake in the morning for, someone to nurture, someone to love."

"And this Fred is it." Mom's voice dripped with suspicion. "He has a son-in-law, so at least one daughter. Does he have a wife?"

"His wife died three years ago. He's been questing for purpose ever since. His children—he has three—keep trying to fill the gap, but they're grown with families and lives of their own."

I couldn't stop myself from asking, "If he was your first love, what happened? Why didn't you marry him instead of Thomas?"

"Oh, my." Dotty shook her head. "It's a long story, but basically, the timing was wrong. After a truly magical summer together, fall arrived and he went off to college. We swore nothing would change, and it didn't, for a while. I visited him a few times with my mother as chaperone, but by Christmas, he'd already grown restive, unsettled about our relationship. He'd begun to chafe at the restrictions of having a distant high school girlfriend. By spring, he was done—sent me a letter breaking things off.

"I was devastated. Could *not* understand it at the time, though it's clear to me now. Took me almost a year to move on. Then, three years later, when I was in college, he called to invite me to a party hosted by his friend. I agreed to go, mostly out of curiosity.

"That was my first experience with time travel. When we entered the party, time rolled back to the summer when we were in love. No one commented on the fact we were together. No one asked where I'd been for three years. The same couples, the same music, same conversations—*everything* was unchanged except my memories.

"Time caught up to us when we sat talking in Fred's car. He had a reunion in mind, but I said no. There was someone else in my life. We made the let's-be-friends resolution, which didn't last a day. When I called the next morning, Fred brushed me off; I'd wounded him with my rejection. About a year later, I got an invitation to his out-of-town wedding, which hurt, because it seemed so final."

"With respect," I said, "Fred doesn't sound like a very nice person."

"You have to remember how young we were. We had no idea how to handle complex emotions. But, mostly, the timing was off." She eyed me closely before her gaze rose to Tyler. "Surely, the two of you know how that is."

Nonplused, I squirmed in my seat while my mother's head jerked in our direction. She stared, then said, "You two? You're a couple?"

Tyler put his hand on my shoulder. "A work in progress."

Dotty laughed. "At last. You were so blind to Megan as a teen. I'm glad your eyes are open now."

"So am I." Tyler squeezed my shoulder.

"What if Fred isn't what he seems?" Mom asked. "What if he's after your money?"

"We knew our families would assume we'd fallen into the clutches of a gold digger," Dotty said. "That's the real reason we didn't get in touch with anyone. We needed time to decide if what we felt was just nostalgia or the start of something new. Could we be happy with each other at this age? Quite a weighty decision, not to be made while our loving relations insisted we part ways to 'save' us from ourselves."

"And?" I pressed. "Are you happy with each other?"

"We think so. We think so enough to make a plan to live together at his home in Boston and see how things go."

"You came to that conclusion awfully quickly," Mom said.

"I married Thomas after knowing him only two weeks. Best decision of my life. I trust my instincts, Allison."

"What about Spear Point?" Tyler asked.

"I'm bequeathing Spear Point to you and to Allison jointly in my will, but I don't intend to die anytime soon. I'll need a caretaker for the house most of the year, though I'd like to spend at least part of each summer here. What do you say, Megan? Would you accept a paid housekeeper position? Your mother told me some time ago you were looking for a job."

"Me? A housekeeper? Uh...I don't know. I should be getting my law credentials in order, and—"

"You can do so here in Maine unless you'd rather be in Florida."

I shook my head, focusing on Dotty, afraid to look Mom in the eye. "I'm grateful my parents let me live with them, but I don't think Florida is where I belong."

"Maine's a good choice," Dotty said. "Lots of opportunity for young people here. And, while you're waiting for the credentialling process to wind up, you can make a rather nice living from commissions earned by disposing of my collections. It's time I pass on those items to others. Storing them serves no purpose. Have you investigated the collections?"

My mind reeled. She'd trust me with such incredible things? I tried to be nonchalant. "I saw the boxes in the shed and had a look at your inventory, but I know nothing about antiques, collectibles, stuff like that. I'm afraid I'd let you down."

Dotty tapped her forehead. "You're intelligent. You can learn.

Sam, at the antique shop in town, can be a big help."

She was right. Still, I had to know, "Where did all those valuables come from? As a teacher, how could you afford them?"

"Thomas. He was a genius at investing. Bought Microsoft, Nvidia, and Apple when they were new. He had his eye on Amazon, but they didn't go public until after his death. I bought the initial public offering. Didn't want to keep all the profits in stock, so I purchased collectibles."

Mom rolled her eyes. "And I was worried about your finances."

"My finances are fine, and so are Fred's. He worked as an investment banker in Boston during the boom years of business consolidations."

The front door opened. Dad and Fred came in. Dad peeked into the parlor, looking uncertain. "Okay for us to come in now?" he asked.

"Yes." Dotty patted the seat beside her and beckoned to Fred, taking his hand when he joined her. "How do you like Spear Point?" she asked him.

"It's lovely. Very relaxing."

"Except when Dotty's missing," Tyler quipped. His tone was friendly and unoffensive, meant to be a joke, which is how everyone took it, but he'd reminded me of the calamitous day we had.

I looked up at him. "Uh, Ty, can we have a word in private?" I hoped we could devise a way to keep Dotty from spotting the mess in the kitchen, the hole in the study wall.

Too late. Dotty said, "We should have some refreshments. I'll make tea," and she left the parlor heading toward the kitchen.

We heard her footsteps pause, start again, stop, then a cry. "Oh, no!" A moment later, she was back, her face aghast, asking plaintively, "What has happened to my house?"

I would have told Dotty all the details of the break-in, Colin hiding in the cellar, our suspicions Colin and Chloe were kidnappers, our attempts to get into the Secret Room, and Eric's duplicity about the runestone. Tyler kept things simple.

He said, "I had a stalker, a woman named Chloe Goode, who became obsessed with me after one date. She convinced herself we were soulmates and made my life hell in Portland. When I moved to Spear Point, I figured I'd shaken her off, but she found out I was here. She finagled a way to reach Spear Point on Eric Lundgren's boat. Colin Currie was with them."

"You reconnected with Erik and Colin?" Dotty cut in. "What are those boys doing these days?"

"Erik's a detective, and Colin's an archaeologist. Colin is heading up a local expedition to find Viking artifacts. And, as it turns out, the stone Megan's brother found by the grotto has immense historical importance. People will want to scrutinize the place it came from."

"That would be the shoal just off Spear Point," Dotty said. "Thomas told me the grotto builders took stone from the shoal to elevate the grotto walls."

"Oh!" I tugged at Tyler's hand and looked up at him. "No worries about an invasion of strangers. The shoal's only above water at low tide, so anyone wanting to search for more Viking inscriptions will have to come by boat. You can give Colin the stone."

Tyler asked Dotty, "He'd like to study the stone and publish his findings. Would that be all right?"

"Certainly. I always did like Colin."

So, one issue resolved. How to tell Dotty about breaking into the Secret Room and bashing a hole in the wall?

Once again, Tyler summarized neatly. "Back to what I was saying: This woman, Chloe, decided to kidnap me. She had a gun.

After locking Colin in the cellar, she marched Erik and me to the boat house to wait out a fog. She didn't know Megan was in the house—actually, Megan was in the cellar. Megan and Colin opened a hatch in the cellar wall by finding a key—"

"*The* key?" Dotty leaned forward, eyes gleaming. "I've been searching for a key in the garden for years."

"If you mean the one from Thomas' letter, it was never in the garden," I said. "The key was in aa wall near the cistern because biblical gardens were places of abundant water. When we opened the hatch, Colin crawled into the space under the stairs and found Hiram Miller's pirate treasure. Unfortunately, Colin had to break through the study wall to get free and rescue Tyler."

"The treasure's worth a lot," Tyler added. "Around a million dollars."

"Oh, my word!" Dotty threw her head back and moaned, "Thomas, you were far too clever." Then, she looked at me. "You deciphered the clue. You had his letter. Where was it? I'd lost it."

"The letter was in a book you donated to the library. The librarian thought you'd want it back. I used the letter to figure out how to get into the Secret Room because we thought we might trade valuables there with the kidnapper to ransom you."

"Yeah," said Tyler bleakly. "We tried to get in but failed. The doors only open a few inches."

"Well, you need to insert a quarter in the gap under the track about four feet to the right of center where the door sticks," Dotty informed him.

"A quarter," Tyler repeated in disbelief.

"Mm. Always works. I'll show you in a bit, once I hear what happened with this crazed woman."

Tyler explained how I'd posed as a ghost using flour as part of my disguise and how the distraction let Colin capture Chloe. “After that, sheriff’s deputies hauled Chloe away. Would have been fine except for Erik getting shot in the arm. He’ll be okay.”

“Shot!” Mom hissed, “Jason, I k*new* there was more going on here than Megan told us on the phone. Something just wasn’t right.”

“You did,” he agreed. “Mother instincts are never wrong.” Dad gave me a hard look, but I saw pride in his eyes, too. “Posing as a ghost for an armed woman was a strange strategy and a risk, Megs.”

I shrugged.

Fred told Dotty, “I think we’ll be safer in Boston.”

“Unless your children decide to shoot me for stealing their dad,” she tossed off. To the rest of us, Dotty said, “We’re staying here overnight, then it’s down to Boston to talk with Fred’s relatives. I’m not looking forward to their objections.”

“It’ll be all right, Dot,” Fred said. “Your family’s taken the news rather well, I think.” And he graced us with a grateful smile. “Thank you for listening, and for respecting our decisions. I promise to take good care of Dotty.”

He was an old man to me, but at that moment, I saw the bedroom eyes Dotty described and felt their allure. I heard a voice sooth me into trust. I liked Fred, and I believed in Dotty’s instincts.

17.

I needed a break. I think everyone did.

Dotty went off toward the kitchen with Fred at her heels. Mom and Dad settled on the front porch. Through the window, I saw worry on Mom's face. Dad looked thoughtful.

I headed for Dotty's bedroom. Tyler followed, asking, "What are we doing in here?"

"Clearing out my things and tidying up for Dotty. Maybe Fred, too. Do you think they're sleeping together?"

"At their age?" Tyler rubbed his chin. Then he shrugged. "No clue."

I moved the soiled dress to a chair and then grabbed my clothes from wherever I'd tossed them to shove into my suitcase. "Strip the bed," I ordered Tyler.

Pulling out the drawer at the base of the left armoire, where the linens were stored, I chose a set of sheets with small rosebuds smelling pleasantly of lavender. I snatched up fluffy, white bath towels, as well.

Tyler asked, "Why is it that whenever we have something important to discuss there's a wad of bedding in the way?" He dropped the sheets on the floor. "Come here." He sat and patted the bed beside him.

I put the linens on the bed and sat staring forward, not looking at him.

"What's wrong? You're in the same frenzied mood you were in

when you thought Colin and I were plotting to steal from Dotty."

I blew air through my lips. "I…I'm overwhelmed, confused. So relieved Dotty's safe. Glad she's happy, but she's rearranged my entire life. What if I can't do what she wants? What if living here is a mistake?"

"*Mistake*? It's perfect. We have all the time we want to be together." Tyler held my hand. "I feel like it's Christmas and birthday rolled into one, don't you?"

When I didn't answer, he added, "Unless…that's not what you want."

"I don't know. It's all happened so fast. Maybe we just got wrapped up in the crisis. I mean, what if we decide we're all wrong? How awkward would it be stuck on an island together after a break up?"

"You're overthinking."

"I wish I'd thought more before marrying Chase. I wish—"

Tyler shifted his position to sit facing me. I turned to see him better. "Look, everyone makes mistakes. I did. I thought Nicole was the one, but she wasn't." He shook his head, then regarded me with soulful eyes. "We've learned, grown up. This is different. You and I. It's somehow meant to be."

He touched my cheek, saying gently, "If people old as Dotty and Fred can take a chance on each other, why should we be cowards? And, today, you risked your life for me. Don't turn Scaredy Cat again." He waited with a mixture of fear and hope on his face, the beautiful, dimpled, blue-eyed face I knew I'd never tire of seeing.

I kissed him. A surge of desire washed over me over me from roots of hair to toes. I was breathless when the kiss ended.

Tyler murmured, "That's a good start. Let's make the future be what we want it to be." He leaned in to kiss me again.

The door opened. "Oh!" Dotty said. "I'll come back."

"No. No, uh, it's all right." I separated from Tyler to sit primly on the bed's edge. "Is there something we can do for you?"

"Well, when you have time, I thought I'd like to see the pirate treasure."

"Of course," Tyler said. "I can't wait to see the Secret Room doors open."

Dotty stepped into the bedroom. "I know I had a coin just the right size somewhere here. Um…." She stared at her dresser. "Yes. It's in the sock drawer."

While Dotty went to get the coin, Tyler and I stood, shaking our heads. After everything we'd tried to gain entry to the Secret Room, the answer was in Dotty's sock drawer.

She reached into the dresser, pulling her hand free holding a coin, a triumphant smile on her face. But when she spotted her soiled dress in the corner, she went to have a look, lifting the once-white lacy bodice.

My heart sank. Now, she'd lay into me, for sure. Or worse.

Instead, I heard, "Don't fret about the dress. I have so many others—all yours, now, if you want them."

Gawking at her, I must have looked unhinged because she laughed. "Really. I must get a new wardrobe for Boston. Here, people know me, but I can't have Fred's friends and relatives think he's living with a madwoman."

"No! Your beautiful clothes. They're your signature, your identity. You can't give them up."

"Megan, dear, clothes are no one's identity. We change them when we change. I'll be the same…." She tapped her chest. "Inside. Now, let's go see that treasure."

I trailed after Dotty and Tyler as we left the bedroom. Dotty stopped in the parlor to glance out the window, giving Fred and my parents a cheerful wave. Apparently, he'd gone outside to join them on the porch. "Oh, dear," she muttered when she turned back to us. "We'll have to hurry with the treasure viewing. I can't leave Fred to Allison's tender mercies too long. She'll grill him like a police detective."

"She loves you," I said loyally, again following in her wake.

Dotty paused at the entrance to the dining room. "I know. I'm blessed to have such a fine family."

"You might not feel so grateful after inspecting the study," Tyler warned. "But don't worry. I can fix it."

"You said Colin broke through the wall to save you. That's what matters." Dotty entered the study, glanced at the piles of books and then crossed to the bookcases concealing the Secret Room. She beckoned to Tyler. "Could you put the coin in place? My knees don't like scrabbling around on the floor."

He took the coin Dotty offered, inspecting it before kneeling at the spot she indicated. "It's old." Studying it more closely, he said, "The date's 1910."

"It's a 1910 Barber quarter with liberty head and eagle," Dotty confirmed.

"Is it rare?" Tyler asked.

"It is, but go ahead and use it."

He stretched out to slide the coin beneath the case, conferring with Dotty to get it positioned correctly. When she nodded, he got to his feet.

"Megan, you know how to operate the desk?" Dotty asked.

"I do. It's—"

"Wait. I need to know something first. I take it you were sleeping in my room because you're uncomfortable in your old room, the nursery. Are you still afraid of our ghost?"

"Not at all." I started moving the desk drawers to set the bookshelf mechanism in motion. "I think Amanda's here to protect us, or, well, her descendants like Tyler."

"Good. That's good. At least, you won't be appalled by what you see in the Secret Room."

I stopped with my hand on the last drawer. *Appalled?* We'd seen most of the room through Tyler's phone camera, but the back corner, the one where a mysterious white blur spoiled the shot.... Could there be something gruesome in the dark space—a mummy, a skeleton, one of those pictures of people dressed to go out except their dead eyes were closed?

Nah. Dotty wouldn't do something so macabre. Of course, she wouldn't.

I eyed Dotty. She was grinning at me. Pulling the last desk drawer out, I heard the Secret Room motor power up, watched the doors part, and keep going. They passed the obstacle that always caused a hitch before. When each door reached the adjoining wall, the motor sound cut off. Before us, an inky doorway yawned like a toothless mouth.

Dotty moved into the room without hesitation, reaching down for the basket of pirate coins. A greenish light positioned somewhere on the floor turned on, illuminating her path to the desk. She switched on the lamp, and sat to look at the hoard. Tyler stood beside her, explaining what we knew about the coins.

I looked toward the far corner. If there were anything appalling in this room, it had to be there. Still bathed in shadow, the dark place waited. I moved toward it. Tyler was right: I wanted no more of my Scaredy Cat days.

Light jumped out of the corner. I flinched, then realized there was another motion-activated lamp. This one stood above a chintz-covered, floral easy chair set beside a round table with a fringed tablecloth. The table held framed photos and a vase of silk flowers. I stood in the cozy corner, then turned, perplexed, to Dotty.

She left her desk and came to stand beside me. "It's for Amanda. I heard somewhere ghosts liked a spot where the living won't bother them, a refuge, so to speak." Touching the frames, swiping at dust, she wrinkled her nose. "Must clean in here more often."

"These are…what?" I asked, pointing to the photos.

"They're images of her family, all I could find. See here? These are her three children as children and as adults. The son who died in the mental hospital, well, I just have a picture of him as a boy. The others are her grandchildren, great-grandchildren and so on." Dotty lifted a picture from the back of the group.

I clapped my hand to my chest. Tyler! There was Tyler as a teen, smirking, just as I remembered him.

"Need to update this one, don't I?" Dotty murmured. "He's not a boy anymore. And," she raised an eyebrow at me, "I'll have to make space for his future children."

"You're not being subtle."

"Can't be. I'm too pleased you two have given each other a second chance, and I'll get to see you often. That is…" She turned serious. "You are staying, aren't you?"

"I am. And I thank you for the opportunity."

"Tush. No need to be formal. We're family." Dotty reached an arm around my waist, and we walked back to the Secret Room entrance together.

"What did I miss?" Tyler asked. He had the treasure basket in hand. "In the corner, I mean."

"Family memorabilia. You're taking the coins out of here?"

"To show your parents and Fred."

“Oh, and I want my pearls.” Dotty headed for the jewelry armoire.

I thought about all the speculation people had had about what was in this room. No one guessed it was a ghost retreat.

The day wound down with conversation, a meal Tyler and I cooked together, and coffee or tea. Mom and Dad seemed satisfied, at last, that Fred was a good guy. Dotty and Fred were simply happy. I finished straightening up in Dotty’s bedroom, moved my things to the hall, and then set up the guest room for my parents. We ended the day with a group stroll along the shore to let the waves calm the last of our worries and the stars give promise to another day.

When our elders went to the house, Tyler asked, “You ready for a ghostly night in the nursery?”

I slipped my arms around his neck. “Better not chance it.”

“My cottage is safe,” Tyler ventured.

“Sounds like the place to be.” I stepped back to take his hand, and we walked together into our future.

About the Author

Sanna Hines writes stories set in the thin places—where the past presses close and the present is never the whole story

She lives in coastal Maine in a town dating from 1623 and generations of former residents are still part of local memory. Her novels explore the subtle magic that emerges in landscapes shaped by centuries of human presence. She's always loved history, but never before had a chance to live in it.

Her writing journey began with studies in journalism, art history and business, leading to a career in marketing communications. Later, she turned to fiction.

Sanna embroiders, makes costumes, and holds two black belts in Tae Kwon Do.

Follow Sanna on

Amazon, Facebook, Goodreads, BookBub, Tumblr, Instagram and her website https://sannahines.wixsite.com/sanna-hines-worlds/.

If you enjoyed this book, please review. All reviews are deeply appreciated.

More from Sanna Hines

Stealth Moves

Boston students and a novice bodyguard face a kidnapper with two souls.

Shining Ones: Legacy of the Sidhe

Irish myth meets modern world as the Tuatha de Danann combat ancient foes for the chance to live and love forever.

Elvira Wonders

The town of Elvira is home to creatures the world doesn't want—or wants too much. In a place full of monsters, how do you find a killer?

Kor and the Wingless Stranger

Kor has five days to save his village, help a lost stranger, and impress a haughty girl.

Tyme & Tyde

Rooted in the forgotten history of New England in the 1600s, *Tyme & Tyde* is a tale of love, danger, and the strange inheritance that binds one woman to time itself in a richly atmospheric work of dual timeline historical fiction.

www.ingramcontent.com/pod-product-compliance
Lightning Source LLC
LaVergne TN
LVHW090954080826
845145LV00003B/1004